THE BREATH
OF FREEDOM

Thank you
Sam Paolucci

THE BREATH OF FREEDOM

SALVATORE (SAM) PAOLUCCI

iUniverse, Inc.
Bloomington

THE BREATH OF FREEDOM

Copyright © 2011 by Salvatore Paolucci.

All rights reserved. No part of this book may be used or reproduced by any means, graphic, electronic, or mechanical, including photocopying, recording, taping or by any information storage retrieval system without the written permission of the publisher except in the case of brief quotations embodied in critical articles and reviews.

iUniverse books may be ordered through booksellers or by contacting:

iUniverse
1663 Liberty Drive
Bloomington, IN 47403
www.iuniverse.com
1-800-Authors (1-800-288-4677)

Because of the dynamic nature of the Internet, any web addresses or links contained in this book may have changed since publication and may no longer be valid. The views expressed in this work are solely those of the author and do not necessarily reflect the views of the publisher, and the publisher hereby disclaims any responsibility for them.

Any people depicted in stock imagery provided by Thinkstock are models, and such images are being used for illustrative purposes only.
Certain stock imagery © Thinkstock.

ISBN: 978-1-4620-6710-7 (sc)
ISBN: 978-1-4620-6711-4 (ebk)

Printed in the United States of America

iUniverse rev. date: 11/18/2011

CONTENTS

Chapter 1	The Children	1
Chapter 2	The Plan	5
Chapter 3	The Papers	8
Chapter 4	The Journey Begins	13
Chapter 5	Amsterdam	17
Chapter 6	The Breath Of Freedom—America	23
Chapter 7	A New Home	27
Chapter 8	The Consulate	34
Chapter 9	The Letter	40
Chapter 10	The Practice	51
Chapter 11	A Great Find	62
Chapter 12	Nadya's Discovery	68
Chapter 13	Discovered	74
Chapter 14	Nadya's Dream	78
Chapter 15	A New Heading	88
Chapter 16	The Permanent Patient	93
Chapter 17	The Turning Point	101
Chapter 18	Family	108
Chapter 19	The New Arrivals	111
Chapter 20	Woman Of The Year	117

PROLOGUE

MY FATHER, GEROG YAKOV

A week after my tenth birthday father had come home from work early. He appeared tense and nervous. He hugged me and kissed me on both cheeks just as he always did. He walked back to the door, opened it and checked the hallway. He walked over to me, turned around and walked back to the door, opened it, and looked up and down the hall again. Father then went to the window, looked down at the street, and then closed the heavy window curtain. He crossed over to the table and sat down.

He pulled up a chair next to his, patted the seat, and gestured for me to sit down. For a long time he just looked at me. Then he began.

"Yakov, I was there. As a fervent twenty two year old revolutionary, I was there. In the streets of Petrograd I led riots, organized strikes, and spoke at meetings about the virtues of the Bolshevik party. I was there and with all my heart and soul I believed in the party. By the end of October, 1917, we had defeated all of the various factions that once struggled for power. I was there through it all. And in the end I proudly stood by Vladimir Lenin's side, as he became the leader of all of Russia. Now all of the dreams for a new Russia that the Bolsheviks had proposed could be brought to fruition."

He stopped, got up from his chair and checked the hallway again. He returned to his chair.

"Papa", I said, "I have to go pee."

He smiled for the first time since he had come home.

"Go," he said.

I walked to the door, opened it, and looked up and down the hall just like papa had done. No one was there so I proceeded to the toilet. I could make no connection to what he had told me. The only thing that I understood was that it was important to him.

My father, Gerog Yakov, began loving me while I was still in my mother's uterus. I swear that I could feel his love through the touch of his hands when momma would let him feel my movements inside her. And in my infancy I grew to love him. The bond that ties a father and son together has probably existed since the beginning of man's emergence on this planet. But as I grew older I sensed that something was troubling him. Somehow I knew that it had nothing to do with me. Whatever it was it never diminished his love for me or my love for him.

My father was a member of the Politburo, the Russian parliament. He was a low level member of the communist party. For his part in helping the Bolshevik party rise to power in the 1917 revolution he was rewarded with a lifetime job.

As the years passed my papa had become disillusioned with the party. The empty promises that once fueled his passion for a better life for the Russian people still echoed in his mind. The only change that my father saw was the corruption that had ensnared the top members of the party. For the ordinary Russian nothing had changed. The fear of death for any infraction by anyone was the only reality of each and every day. Even my father was not exempt from that fear. His position in the government was no insulation from death.

As I grew into adulthood I began to feel the same oppression that my parents had lived with for over twenty years. As a child they had sheltered me from it. But as my environment expanded the feeling of utter helplessness crept into me like a spreading cancer. Papa kept promising me that someday I would have a better life. He kept telling me that he had a plan. He promised that when the time was right he would tell Momma and me what it was. That promise was the only thing that kept hope alive in both of us.

To dearest papa prosperity for all and power to the people had not been just empty words. But after the fires of revolution had dwindled papa became more of a realist. He knew that all the wonderful changes that the party was going to bring to the people would take time to implement. Even after the assassination of Lenin and Josef Stalin's rise to power, he was still hopeful that change would come. But as the years passed realism changed to cynicism, and by 1938, the only change that had happened was hope no longer existed in him. It was replaced by horror and an oppression that was so vicious and cruel that no one, absolutely no one, felt safe in any way. No one dared to speak of it. If you did your voice was never heard again.

Josef Stalin had thousands of people killed. He had become so paranoid that he saw plots to kill him everywhere. Even a rumor of someone's involvement to eliminate him could bring death.

By the year 1938, my father had not risen very far in the party ranks. His disenchantment was now complete. Now he saw clearly what his party had become, what it really was. It was the party of doom, utter despair, and death.

Many of the top people who had great power in the military and the communist party were making decisions that affected many lives. Those judgments were coming from minds totally clouded by booze. Everyone drank heavily. My father's disenchantment was felt by many of the party leaders. But they never dared to speak of it openly so they drank to dull the anguish and the pain of failure.

For the peasants of Russia nothing had changed. Oppression was nothing new to them. Most could not read or write and in their ignorance they lived out their lives. To their leaders the common ordinary peasant was of no more importance than a blade of grass. What was left for the party faithful? They too had lost hope. But they dared not object or ask questions. If anyone did, a bullet or the rope was his or her reward. The Gulag prisons were filled with many brave dissenters. As a result of the fear of dying the bureaucrats and the military leaders turned to drinking. Booze numbed their guilt and they kept on breathing for another day.

My father had been a fervent believer in the Bolshevik revolution. He was a dedicated party member that did whatever was asked of him. Papa gradually rose through the lower ranks of the party. This gave him the impression that he was going somewhere within the party. In reality he was a very minor player. He found himself falling into the role of the "go-to guy". If a minister wanted fine whiskey, talk to Gerog. If a visiting dignitary from a government favorable to the Russian cause who was seeking carnal delights, talk to Gerog Yakov. In this role he could provide whatever titillating desire any man could want. Even the name of a hit man was included in the ask Gerog list. But if it were possible Gerog would secretly send an anonymous message warning the intended victim. How to set up a secret account for any superior that might ask was not an unusual request. By keeping his mouth shut and his eyes open he learned where many of the bodies were buried. This made his disillusionment almost intolerable to bear. The only thing that kept him focused each day was the plan. The plan that was slowly forming in his mind gave him a new sense of purpose. He now looked at each odorous request differently. Was there something in a request that he could use in his plan to save his son?

At one time he had wanted to quit the party but he knew that if he did it would draw unwanted attention To himself. So he did the next best thing. My father, Gerog Yakov, started keeping a secret journal. He entered names, dates, and how much money was involved in each transaction.

My papa neither smoked nor drank so his mind was always clear. He knew all too well what drinking could do to the human mind. Dealing with inebriated clients was almost a daily occurrence. As the go-to guy he was constantly juggling events, names, dates, and times. Clarity was essential. The same passion that my father once had for the party was now directed toward only one goal. He was going to get my family and me out of Russia to a new life of freedom in America.

Papa desperately wanted to save me from this evil society. It had become a society that systematically turned a human mind to mush and wrapped the heart in barbed wire. He knew if anyone even suspected that he was plotting to get us out of Russia it would be a death sentence for all of us. In the late summer of 1938, my father, Gerog Yakov, put his plan of escape for us into action.

CHAPTER 1

THE CHILDREN

It was thirteen years ago that young Yakov Yakov had sat beside his papa. He had not understood the ramblings of his father on that day. But with each slowly passing year Yakov began to understand the full meaning of what his father had said. Now as the adult Yakov, standing before the cracked lavatory mirror, he saw in his reflected eyes the same hopelessness and despair that he saw in his father's eyes. He and his wife, Nadya, and their two-year-old son, shared a small upstairs two-bedroom apartment with Yakov's parents. But the stinking lavatory at the end of the hall was shared with other tenants in the decrepit state-owned apartment. He felt as if his soul was being violated having to share his reflection with so many people. Many that he didn't even know. He wondered if they saw what he saw in the dingy mirror. He was looking into the eyes of a very confused 23-year-old young man. There was no hope in the eyes of his reflection. He could see only the fear of death that his father and mother had lived with for so long.

His muscular six-foot athletic body was barely discernable under the drab loosely fitting clothes that almost all of the citizens of Moscow wore. The young women of Moscow didn't notice his apparel but they certainly were attracted to the strong chiseled features of his face. Nadya, his wife, often teased Yakov

1

about the extra glances that he drew from the young ladies. She never showed any jealousy. His wife enjoyed watching him blush whenever she pointed to some giggling young girls as they looked at him.

He had completed a three year course at The Moscow Institute of Chiropractic. His parents had never heard of this kind of schooling. They knew that it had something to do with the human body. That was all.

Yakov was aware that many people had never heard of it. But he was sure that he could convince people of the value of his services. Finding a place to open up an office was proving to be difficult. Even with his father's connections no one wanted to venture into the new science. Yakov had heard that chiropractics was becoming popular in France. But the French were known to be a touchy feely people in general. They were more open about the human body. Yakov's venture into love helped ease the anguish of being unemployed. The sexual attraction that they both felt so strongly was hard to keep under control. Society dictated that they wait until they were married. But their passion was so much stronger than societal mores. Their love was consummated a week after they had met.

Nadya had been instantly drawn to him from the moment she looked into his eyes when they first met. Yes, she saw the handsome features, but there was a quality about him that attracted her more deeply than what was on the surface. She sensed his compassion. She didn't see the confusion that was occupying so much of his thoughts. They lived in a society that was supposed to have created a utopia for all its citizens. But instead, the dreams of equality for all turned into a nightmare of repression for everyone. The tiniest attempt at changing anything would be crushed by the brutal totalitarian government. All the power was in the hands of one man, Josef Stalin. He saw plots to kill him everywhere. Because of his paranoia thousands were killed, even Stalin's own childhood friend. Yakov struggled with these events. The breath of Russia was being squeezed out of every single citizen. Yakov knew that some how they had to escape. Deep within him was this silent dilemma that he could not speak of. He did not dare to speak of this to anyone, not even to Nadya. Outwardly she saw only the confidence and self-esteem that was evident to her in the language that his body spoke. Every movement that he made, the way he walked, the way he showed compassion for others. This is what sparked the feelings in her that turned into the love that became so deeply embedded in her heart.

Nadya remembers the day that they met. She was attending the Moscow Institute of Medicine. Few women were given the privilege of attending the famous Russian school. Her father, General Tchaikovsky, had great favor with the Prime Minister, Josef Stalin. But in the Russian bureaucracy favor was often followed by failure. In 1935, General Tchaikovsky was executed, along with eight other high ranking officers. Her father was accused of plotting to overthrow the government. The evidence against him was scant to non—existent. Just the rumor of his involvement was all that Stalin needed. Her mother could not stand the shunning and loneliness that grew within her day by day. She hung herself on the 31st of December, six months to the day that her husband had died. Their only child, Nadya, grieved for them everyday. Death was a fact of life. People disappeared everyday. Fear was a constant companion in every person's life. But she continued with her studies. Even as she carried that same fear, she could never understand why those in power allowed her to stay in school. When a man of power fell from grace, invariably, the entire family was punished. She did not know that one of her professors had pleaded with a high-ranking member of the politburo to let her finish her studies. The professor had told him she was one of the finest students he had ever seen and that Russia needed people like her. To dismiss her from the program would be a terrible waste. To everyone's surprise he agreed. The real reason for the fat little man's decision was the professor was now indebted to him. The more favors people owed him the safer he felt.

Let's suppose that the obese bureaucrat needed a vial filled with a lethal potion to eliminate a threat to his own safety. How easy it would be for a professor with hospital privileges to get him something without raising any suspicion. You had to protect your own ass from a constant barrage of attacks whether they were real or imagined and trying to find the distinction between the two is what sustained the high consumption of vodka.

CHAPTER 2

THE PLAN

Systematically over the years Gerog had begun to accumulate rubles. Whenever he had been asked to satisfy a request a modest price was attached to the deal. The amount was kept small so as not to attract suspicion. Asking for ten rubles didn't raise an eyebrow. His superiors looked upon it as a token amount for services rendered. They considered ten rubles for his services a pittance for what Gerog often provided.

Whenever diplomats returned from foreign assignments Gerog knew that they often returned with a stash of American currency. In clandestine transactions American money was often used. One glimpse of the greenbacks and the deal was sealed. Gerog would often ask that a few American dollars be included in his payment for his services along with the ten rubles. Again, the amount was always small, never more than two or three dollars. The joke among the diplomatic corps was that Gerog was saving up for an early retirement in the west.

By the end of 1937, Yakov's father, Gerog, had saved over a thousand rubles and almost 375 American dollars. The dollars were much more valuable than the Russian rubles.

This part of his plan had been easy. Now he was ready to embark on phase two. By this time a problem that had been developing had reached epic proportions. Yakov's wife, Nadya, had developed an addiction to pain medication. During the birth of their son, complications developed. Her uterus had detached from the interior wall of the lower abdomen. Her doctor had tried to suture the organ back in place but only succeeded in making matters worse. The pain was not totally debilitating and she was able to get something for it at the medical school she was attending. Nadya's condition was an event that Gerog later turned into an asset.

In the spring of 1938, Gerog asked everyone in the family to meet with him in the apartment. Gerog's Paranoia was increasing. He tightly pulled the heavy drapes that were used to keep out the winter cold, over all the windows. He opened the locked door that led into the hall to see if anyone was there. Quietly he closed the door and returned to the others. Slowly he started to explain to his family the extreme disillusionment that had come into his mind. The party that he once thought was the hope for all mankind had become a playground for the elite few at the top of the party. From Stalin on down, they used their power to consolidate their positions. And that power was used ruthlessly to control everything.

"I am going to get you, Nadya, and Sergi to America," said Gerog.

Yakov and Nadya could not believe what his father was proposing. His mother, Evet had already been told of the plan. She had agreed with Gerog, even though her heart already grieved for them. She would not stand in the way of a better life for them and her grandson.

Yakov looked at his father in total disbelief. "How do you plan to do this", asked Yakov?

He knew if the plan failed the result would be the death of his father, humiliation for his mother and Nadya, and prison for him.

Yakov pleaded desperately with his father, "You must give up this idea. If you fail, you and I could be put to death. Give up this insane idea."

Gerog quietly responded by telling Nadya and Yakov that he was determined and that they should be ready to leave at a moments notice. He would have their papers ready in two weeks. Tears streamed down their faces as they embraced each other. Yakov began to believe that a new beginning in a new place called America could end the despair that clouded his mind. Yet, the thought of leaving his parents ripped his soul apart.

Nadya and Yakov left the kitchen and went to their bedroom. They began packing the two small bags that Yakov's father had given them. The small bags would give the illusion that they would be returning to Russia. They packed only what they absolutely needed. Even the scarce pictures of his father and mother had to be left behind. Anything that even hinted that they might not return had to be omitted.

CHAPTER 3

THE PAPERS

On the morning of April the 4th, 1938, Gerog entered the office of the Minister of Diplomatic Travel precisely at 10 o'clock. He approached the secretary's desk, announced who he was, and requested to see Comrade Nicoli Brezhinski. She got up, entered the minister's office, and announced that Comrade Yakov wished to see him. Comrade Brezhinski came to the door and in a loud voice said, "Comrade Yakov, come in, come in." Gerog sat down in the chair in front of the large desk. It was at this point that Gerog noticed what he had hoped for. On Comrade Brezhinski's desk was a half empty bottle of vodka and an empty glass next to it. It was easy to see that the minister was easing himself down from a long weekend party.

"How is your family Comrade Yakov?", asked the minister? He continued, "Would you like a drink?"

Gerog replied, "No drink for me. Thank you. You ask about my family. That is why I am here."

Even in his alcoholic semi stupor the minister sensed Gerog's grave concern.

"I come to you, comrade, with a request of the greatest urgency. My son's wife has a serious illness that is slowly killing her," said Gerog.

THE BREATH OF FREEDOM

"I don't know of anything that I can do for her," replied the minister.

"For what I am about to ask I will be in your debt for ever. I am asking you to grant diplomatic passports for my son Yakov Yakov, his wife, Nadya, and their son," said Gerog, his voice trembling.

While pouring himself a large drink, Brezhinski replied, "Are you out of your mind"? He began pacing the floor.

"Please listen to me. I beg you, listen to me," Gerog pleaded. "She can get the treatments she needs only in America, or she will be dead in a year. You can save her."

"Under what pretext could I possibly send them to America with diplomatic passports", he yelled.

"The reason is logical. They will be going on a fact-finding mission to study the American medical system. She has a medical degree from The Moscow Institute of Medicine. While there she will get the treatment she needs and she can study American medical practices at the same time", argued Yakov. Another drink is poured.

"What about her husband. What will he do? Just stand around holding her hand," replied the minister.

"No, no, no. He also has a degree. Yakov will act as her assistant", replies Gerog.

By now the bottle was almost empty. Brezhinski's mind was swirling. He sat down at his desk, opened the bottom drawer, and removed three papers labeled Diplomatic Visa. He called in the secretary and handed the papers to her.

"Fill these out. Comrade Yukov will give you the details. I will sign them in the morning. I don't feel well and I am going home to rest", he said, his speech badly slurred, as he staggered out the door.

The secretary replied, "Yes Comrade Brezhinski. I will have them ready to be signed when you come in tomorrow." He did not reply.

9

"When should I pick up the papers", asked Gerog?

She replied, "I will have them ready by ten o'clock. I do not know what time the minister will be in to sign them".

The secretary returned to her desk. Gerog followed her out. As he was about to sit in the chair in front of her desk, he suddenly turned and headed back into the minister's office. "I forgot my coat and hat", said Gerog. Once inside he turned toward the door to see if she could see him. She was out of his line of sight. Picking up his coat he removed the journal from the inside pocket, the journal that could send so many to the Gulag prisons. Quickly he placed it in the middle of the many dusty books on the highest shelf just behind his desk. He had a smile on his face. Who would ever think of looking here for his book of blood? He returned to his seat next to her desk and began giving her the information that the forms required. When they had finished he quickly returned to his apartment to prepare his family for their departure.

The next day Gerog was at the office by 10:30. To his surprise, Comrade Brezhinski was already there, waiting for him. He pointed to the chair and Gerog sat down. The minister appeared to be totally sober.

"Comrade Gerog, I was up half the night thinking that I had made a terrible mistake. I am sorry but for my own safety, I cannot grant you the visas", he said. Gerog pleaded with him, but he would not reconsider. He picked up the forms and was about to tear them up. Gerog jumped to his feet, reached over the desk, and put his hand on the papers.

"Comrade, I can make you a very powerful man", he said in a very quiet voice. Power was a word that Brezhnev understood.

What do you mean", he said, as Gerog removed his hand." I have kept a journal for the last ten years. All the requests that I have been asked to perform, illegal or immoral, I have recorded them. Names, places, dates, and the event, are written down", whispered Gerog.

"Is the incident," Before Brezhinski could finish the sentence, Gerog replied, "Yes minister, it is in the journal."

About a year ago, late at night, the exact date was recorded in the journal; Comrade Brezhinski summoned Gerog to his Dacha. Upon his arrival, the minister himself met him at the door. He was wearing a robe. He was drunk, and as white as a sheet. Over and over he repeated, "Help me, help me." He grabbed Gerog's arm and hurriedly rushed him up the stairs to his bedroom. Gerog was horrified. Lying in a pool of blood was the body of a naked boy. He looked to be about twelve years old. Brezhinski was a pedophile, but he had never asked Gerog to procure for him. The boy was very thin. During the act of anal intercourse, the minister had torn open the young boy's colon. While the drunken Brezhinski tried to figure out what to do, the boy slowly bled to death.

Trembling, Gerog asked," what do you want me to do?"

"Get him out. Get him out of here. I'll be ruined. Don't tell anyone Gerog. Save me. Save me. I'll do anything you ask," whimpered the minister.

Gerog grabbed a blanket from the bed, wrapped the body in it, carried it far from the house, and buried him just inside the woods.

Until now, neither of them had ever mentioned the death of the boy.

"Minister, I have never spoken of this to anyone. I swear to you, no one knows. It is only in the journal." Gerog continued, "The journal can make you powerful. The secrets that it contains can destroy your enemies. Once my family is safe in America I will give it to you." There was no need to mention what the journal could do for the minister's career. He reached down, opened the bottom drawer and took out a bottle of vodka. He didn't bother with a glass. The minister put the opened bottle to his lips, and took a long hard drink. The alcohol brought color back to his pale face. For a long while he just sat there. Then he slowly picked up the papers and signed them. He held the papers out to Gerog but did not release the papers as Gerog held on to the other end.

"Promise me. He said, on your mother's grave, you will give me the journal."

"When they are safe, the journal will be yours", replied Georg. The minister released the papers. "One more thing, said Gerog. You will receive a letter by diplomatic courier from the consulate in New York. It will be addressed to your office with my name on it. That letter will tell me that they are safe."

"They are never coming back, are they?", asked Brezhinski.

"No, they won't. To help them start their new life I would like a salary advance in the amount of ten thousand rubles and two hundred American dollars", asked Gerog? Gerog was surprised at his reply.

"I'll see what I can do", replied the minister. Gerog turned and left the office with the precious papers in his briefcase.

CHAPTER 4

THE JOURNEY BEGINS

By the time Gerog arrived at the apartment he was out of breath and sweating. He hoped that he had not attracted any attention with his rapid walk. Numerous glances over his shoulder were made to see if he was being followed. On his way home he had stopped at the rail station. Gerog stood out side the terminal for several minutes before he entered. He felt sure that no one was following him. Gerog did not trust Brezhinski. He hated the NKVD secret police. They could swoop him up and send him off to the Gulag prisons with absolutely no warning. He was becoming as paranoid as Brezhinski and Stalin combined.

Speaking in a quiet voice for fear of being overheard, Gerog asked, "When will the next train for Amsterdam be leaving?" The ticket agent understood the need for quiet and quietly informed him, "The next train leaving for Amsterdam will be leaving in two hours from track four. You must show your papers at the gate."

"My son and his family have diplomatic travel papers."

"That's fine, said the agent, but they will still need to present them at the special gate for diplomats. How many will be traveling?"

"Three," replied Gerog. Two adults and a child."

"Traveling under diplomatic passports the tickets are paid for by the state, said the agent. They will be ready at the gate when you arrive."

"Thank you for your help," said Gerog. As Gerog left the station he wanted to run home as fast as he could. But he dared not do that.

Upon his arrival home he rushed into the apartment. He was almost yelling as he opened his door.

"Momma, children, come listen to me." His family had never seen him like this. "Momma, our children are leaving for America." Tears began streaming from everyone's eyes. The hugging would stop for a moment, only to begin again, longer and stronger than before. "Stop. Stop. Stop," whispered Gerog. He ran to the door, slowly opened it, and looked down the hall. No one was there. Quietly he closed the door. "We have only an hour to get to the train. Momma, put some bread and cheese in a sack. Yakov, Nadya, take the baby and your bags and leave for the station now. Momma, you will follow them in fifteen minutes. Fifteen minutes later I will leave," said Gerog. They all knew walking together would be a suspicious act.

When Gerog finally arrived at the station he approached Yakov, Nadya, and the baby. Quietly they said goodbye. Then Momma took her turn. Slowly the three of them approached the man at the diplomatic gate. Yakov gave their names, and showed the diplomatic travel papers to him. Yakov tried not to look nervous as two armed soldiers standing at the gate watched them.

The man at the gate asked Yakov, "What is your final destination?"

Yakov replied, "America. We are going on a diplomatic fact-finding mission to spy on American medicine." The agent did not smile and gave Yakov a stare of disapproval. The two guards smiled.

"You may board the train at gate four," said the agent.

Gerog and Momma watched as the children walked down the long platform. They hugged each other and cried. Tears of joy, sadness, and longing were all intermixed as the hope for a better life for their children welled up in their hearts. Slowly the train pulled out of the station.

Yakov and Nadya settled into the first seats that they came to. The baby had fallen asleep. Nadya, in her weakened condition, could not carry the child any further. Yakov, struggling with the luggage, sat down and moaned. He laid the bags on the opposite seat. He was still fearful that a member of the N.K.V.D., the secret Russian police, would end their escape. So far they were not asked to show their papers. To them everyone looked suspicious. They could not openly show the grief that was tearing at their hearts at this moment of separation. Staying emotionally composed was essential.

Yakov opened the bag that contained the bread and cheese that his mother had packed. Inside the suitcase there was a note and a letter from his father. Yakov was confused. The letter had his father's name on it but it was addressed to Comrade Brezhinski's office at the Kremlin. As he read the note the matter became clear. Upon his arrival in New York City Yakov was to go to the Russian consulate. He was to show his diplomatic papers to the head of the consulate and ask that the letter be included in the next courier mail pouch leaving for Russia. The letter would let his father know that he and Nadya had arrived safely. The note also contained the name and address of a Russian living in New York who had escaped communist tyranny. Gerog concluded with the admonition that Yakov memorize the name and address and then destroy it. This man still had family in Russia. The N.K.V.D. thinks he is dead. If they were to find that he is alive, his family would be made to suffer.

Your freedom will be paid for in blood. Treasure every breath that you take. Yakov understood whose blood his father spoke of. He covered his face with his scarf and wept.

CHAPTER 5

AMSTERDAM

The train ride was long and exhausting for all of them, especially Nadya. When they arrived in Amsterdam, it was 5 a.m. By the time they had cleared Customs it was close to 6 a.m. So far the passports had worked well. On the train, they were asked for their papers only once. No trouble. Boarding a ship might be different. "Where shall we go?" asked Nadya.

Yakov replied, "I don't know." They left the customs office, walked through a high arch, into the main terminal of the station. There they stopped, totally shocked, trembling and speechless. Nadya and Yakov were absolutely stunned at the mayhem. Their son began to cry as he saw the look of terror in his parents' eyes. People were everywhere. They were laughing, crying, talking, seated, standing, running, and walking. Was this what freedom looked like and sounded like? The noise and the hustle and bustle deepened their shock. Oddly the first normal sensation to return was the feeling of hunger. They slowly moved toward a sausage vendor just a few steps away. Yakov ordered in Russian," two sausages, please?"

The vendor knew Yakov was speaking Russian, but what he was saying he did not know. The vendor raised his hand and gestured for Yakov to wait. He walked over to another vendor

17

and returned with the plump little man who was grinning from ear to ear.

He spoke to Yakov in Russian. Yakov wrapped his arms around him and jumped up and down with joy. This man could have been someone evil. He didn't care. His voice was like music to him. His name was Ivan.

Between the bites of sausage, questions poured out of Yakov and Nadya. Finally they asked where they could board a ship for America. Ivan's smile disappeared. "I don't know, said Ivan. But I know where the American embassy is. They are helping people who want to leave Europe, especially the Jews."

"Why are so many people leaving?" asked Yakov.

"Nazi Germany is taking everything that the Jews own. Adolph Hitler has come to power and blames the Jews for all of Germany's problems. No one can stop him", replied Ivan.

"Can you take us to the embassy"? Asked Yakov. "Yes, replied Ivan. But it will soon be dark."

"Is there a place where we can spend the night?" Asked Yakov, Nadya is exhausted and so is our son."

"Of course, grinned Ivan. I have an extra warm bed and I'll fix you a hot Russian supper. Tomorrow you will feel better."

"How can we ever repay you for your kindness"? Asked Yakov.

"Watching the two of you enjoying the breath of freedom is my payment, said Ivan. I remember what those first weeks were like." Yakov couldn't believe what Ivan had just said. His father had used the same expression in the letter he had placed in his suitcase. Tears of joy streamed down Yakov's face.

Yakov, Ivan, and Ivan's wife, Katrina, talked long into the night. Nadya and the boy went to bed right after supper.

"Ivan is always bringing lost souls here, said Ivan's wife. All his family died in St. Petersburg in a fire. Ivan was working at the time. But he is sure it was set by the N.K.V.D."

"But why", asked Yakov. "Who knows? Several men in the factory where he worked disappeared. Maybe one of them said Ivan was in a plot to kill Stalin to save himself. Ivan managed to escape and ended up here in Amsterdam. This is where we met. I too, was a lost soul once." Ivan wept as Katrina told the story. "Let us rest now. We'll talk again tomorrow," said Ivan.

The next morning, after they had eaten, Ivan and Yakov left for the American embassy. It was decided that Nadya and the baby would stay with Katrina.

When they arrived they were astonished to see a long line of people waiting to get in. Most of them were Jews. As they approached the end of the line, a young looking American with a clipboard, asked Yakov his name in Russian. He entered it on the paper. The agent turned to Ivan, smiled at him, and said, "I see you have brought me another one of your lost souls. Does he have any papers?" Yakov handed him the diplomatic travel papers. The young man's smile disappeared as he read the document. "Follow me," he said. They entered a door just left of the main entrance, bypassing the throng standing in line. The agent stopped in front of a door with the name, Chester Blaine, United States Ambassador, painted on it. He gently tapped on the door. A woman opened it. "Wait here," he said, as he entered the room. After what seemed like an eternity, he returned. "You will see the Ambassador now," said the young man. Entering the room, Yakov saw two large flags behind the desk, to the left and right of the man seated. Yakov immediately recognized the American flag, but did not know the other.

The ambassador stood, and with a firm handshake, said in English, "Welcome Mister Yakov", the ambassador hesitated, "Yakov." "Thank you sir," Said Yakov. The translator exchanged their words. "How did you get the same name twice?" asked

Ambassador Blaine. "My mother played a joke on me. She said whenever anyone asked my name, they would remember it," answered Yakov.

Smiling broadly the ambassador replied, "She is a very smart woman." The young clerk interpreted the remark. Yakov smiled. He instinctively liked this man. "How many are traveling with you"?

"My wife and young son," said Yakov. As soon as the interpretation was completed, the Ambassador returned to his desk, and sat down. He looked at the diplomatic passports and studied them for a long time. Yakov sensed the change in his mood. "My wife is a doctor. We will be studying the American medical system, said Yakov. I also have a degree."

"Why did you bring your son? "Asked Ambassador Blaine. Yakov was going to trust his instinct. "Sir! If we get to America we will not be going back. My wife, Nadya, is ill. She could not get the treatment that she needs in Russia. My father will be killed for helping us to escape when they realize we are not coming back. He wanted us to find freedom, to breathe freedom, and raise our son in a free society."

Ambassador Blaine had not become hardened even though he had heard pleas like Yakov's many times. He stood up and again grasped Yakov's hand. "Welcome to America", he said. Yakov didn't need an interpreter. The wide grins on the interpreter's and the ambassador's faces said it all.

"My aide will see to it that you are put on the next ship leaving for New York City in America. Tomorrow, come back here; and he will tell you the name of the ship, where it leaves from, and the time of departure. He will also give you a letter, signed by me, requesting that you be given political asylum. When you arrive in New York, just as soon as you can, take your wife and child to the American Consulate in New York. Give the letter to Andrew Dempsey, the man in charge there. Good luck Yakov Yakov. Your mother was right", said Ambassador Blaine. He smiled and left the room.

Yakov found Ivan seated in the outer office. As soon as Ivan saw the smile on Yakov's face he ran to him. They were both talking and laughing at the same time. The ambassador's aide was also overcome with joy. He told Ivan what they had to do tomorrow. Ivan assured him they would arrive in the morning promptly at ten.

The next day, exactly at the appointed hour, Ivan and Yakov found the ambassador's aide, working the line outside the embassy. From his jacket pocket he removed the envelope and a folded paper. He shook hands with the two men as he handed Yakov the papers. Yakov thanked him profusely for all that he had done.

Immediately upon their arrival at Ivan's home Yakov placed the letter in his suitcase. Everyone gathered in the kitchen. Yakov opened the typewritten note. It said that the Greek freighter Neptune would be leaving from dock seven at noon tomorrow. They were to board the ship at ten o'clock.

When they arrived at the dock the next day they found the Neptune. It was a small freighter. The owner and captain of the ship was a Greek named Dimitri Tarpolis. His thick gray black hair and brown eyes accented his rugged appearance. When he smiled, his huge mustache would stretch across his face. His manner was warm and friendly. But there was no doubt that he was in charge.

He was also very enterprising. He had converted a large section of the main deck into twenty comfortable cabins. The rooms were offered to the highest bidders. There were plenty of Jewish passengers more than willing to pay. People all over Europe were lined up at every major seaport waiting for passage. For them Dooms Day was coming. Every trip back to America the Neptune's cabins were always full.

Yakov presented the three passports to the captain. He had never seen a diplomatic passport. The previous evening, the ambassador's aide had delivered three vouchers to the Greek captain. When the ship arrived in New York he would turn the vouchers in at the Russian Embassy, and he would be paid. Captain Dimitri did not like dealing with Russians. But the dollar amount was blank on each voucher. It was up to the captain to fill it in. He was very generous to himself.

Yakov and Nadya embraced Ivan. What a guardian angel he had turned out to be. Yakov had removed a ten-dollar bill from the money belt beneath his shirt. His father had warned him to be very careful how he spent the American dollars that he had given him. Yakov was sure of this decision. He slipped the money into Ivan's hand as they shook hands for the last time. Ivan protested vigorously, but finally took it. He had never seen American money.

Escorted by a sailor from the Neptune, Yakov and Nadya, carrying the baby, walked up the gangplank to the ship's deck. They would never forget Ivan.

CHAPTER 6

THE BREATH OF FREEDOM—AMERICA

The six-day trip across the Atlantic was uneventful. To help pass the time Yakov would visit with off duty crewmen. He wanted to learn English. One day as Captain Tarpolis walked by them, as he inspected the ship, he heard Yakov say "som of beech". The others in the room laughed. The captain laughed momentarily. Yakov didn't know why everyone was laughing. The captain told the sailors that cuss words might cause problems for Yakov. The laughing stopped.

Yakov had befriended an older Jewish couple in the cabin next door. Aaron Weintraub and his wife, Marta, were Russian Jews. Hitler wasn't the only one persecuting Jews. Stalin had been killing Jews for years, confiscating their property and selling their possessions to loyal members of the party.

They had escaped from Russian persecution in the city of Kiev. Just as Ivan had become their guardian angel, Yakov did what he could to help this couple. They were delighted to find that Yakov spoke Russian. The old couple was being met at the dock by a rabbi. He had been in America for several years. They hoped his English was good, for they were in desperate need of an interpreter.

By 2:45 P.M., on the sixth day, the pilot tug boats had gently pushed the Neptune to it's mooring at Pier 21 in the Hudson

23

River. Captain Tarpolis notified all the passengers that they were welcome to stay on board one more night if they needed to. There would be no extra charge. Inevitably someone would miss a connection, and it would be several days before the ship was loaded with cargo ready for the return trip to Amsterdam.

The Yakovs' stood at the ship's rail. They did not know what to do.

The Weintraub's stood a few feet away. Suddenly they were yelling and shouting to someone below on the dock. They grabbed Yakov and Nadya by the arm and pulled them along to the ramp. They were surprised by the strength of these two deliriously happy people. They had found their Rabbi. At the end of the ramp the old man and his wife dropped to their knees and kissed the dirty wooden planks beneath them. Their search for freedom was over. Like Nadya and Yakov, they could feel the breath of freedom filling their lungs, giving them new hope for the future. Rabbi Horowitz and Yakov helped Aaron and Marta to their feet. They embraced in a mass hug with the tears of joy running down their faces. This scene was repeated over and over every time another ship docked in New York, Newark, Boston, and all the other ports on the east coast. Boatloads of humanity arrived by the thousands to find freedom. Many had skills that helped them to quickly weave themselves into the American fabric. Those who had to learn new skills found opportunities. Every man woman and child wanted to earn the right to say "I am an American". And of the utmost importance to each of them was learning to speak English. They did not abandon their native languages. It was interwoven with English when they searched for a new word.

Yakov and Nadya, in their entire lives, had never experienced this behavior in complete strangers. They were reaching out to unselfishly help others in a time of great need. Rabbi Solomon Horowitz was one of these people. He took the five of them to the synagogue that he had founded four years ago. In the basement he had constructed cubicles with a bed in each and a curtain stretched across the opening. A toilet and shower stood in the corner across the room from the basement stairs. The thin wooden walls and door offered a little privacy. In the remaining space there was a large table, with eight chairs neatly placed around it. Only two of them matched. Two bare light bulbs managed to illuminate the room. It wasn't the Ritz, but it was warm and clean. Mrs. Horowitz made sure of that.

This would be their home, the Yakovs and the Weintraubs, until they found something more permanent. The next day the three men, Yakov, Mr. Weintraub, and the Rabbi, set out to find their own places to call home.

By the third day, with the help of the Rabbi, Aaron Weintraub and his wife had located a cousin. The Weintraubs had wanted a place of their own. But after a long discussion it was agreed that moving in with the cousin for now was the best choice.

Yakov's housing needs were different. To set up his chiropractic practice he needed rooms to work on patients and separate quarters for him and his family. With these requirements a place would be hard to find. The next day he and the Rabbi set out.

They had searched an eight-block radius around the synagogue and found nothing suitable. Leaving the residential area they entered an industrial section of the city consisting of large and small warehouses and abandoned small factories. Attached to the front of a two storied factory was a one-story office addition. From the outside it appeared to have the space to hold several examination rooms for patients and private quarters As well. There were no signs to tell them who the owner was.

"We'll have to go to city hall tomorrow, to the office of deeds and records," said Rabbi Horowitz. "They will tell us the name of the owner."

The next day, after a long search, they finally found the office. The clerk was a typical male bureaucrat. He stunk of cigar smoke and beer. His belly hung over his belt. His food stained shirt and his belly didn't leave much to the imagination of what his favorite pastime was. Smoke from the cigar clenched in his teeth, almost obscured his face.

"What can I do fa yous," he snarled in his New York City slang.

The Rabbi replied," We would like the owner's name of the small empty factory located on the corner at 44th st. and 10th avenue."

"I'll get yous da book. Yous can look fer it. I ain't got da time ta do it," said the clerk. He walked between rows of shelves that must have held hundreds of large Platt books. Each book contained the location of buildings, by street name, the physical size of the building, and the owners name and address. Returning to the counter he slammed the large volume down. Dust flew everywhere. The man must have known the city very well. It was precisely the book they needed. The pages were hand written and laid out by the avenue names first.

Rabbi Horowitz was astonished. "Here it is, he said. It's listed as vacant. The owner is Vincent Lattori. He lives on Stuyvesant Street, 1225."

Yakov asked," how far is it?" His mind was still filled with fear. It was difficult for him to absorb how easily a person could move so freely from place to place in America. There are so many small everyday details in being free in America. It would take Yakov and Nadya many months before the fears that controlled their lives for so many years in Russia would be dispelled.

CHAPTER 7

A NEW HOME

After searching for a while they finally found Mr. Lattori's home. They rang the bell on the door. After what seemed an eternity Mr. Lattori opened the door. He was middle aged, dressed in a neatly tailored three piece suit. His grey speckled black moustache was neatly trimmed. He had neatly well groomed hair, the same color as the hair beneath his nose.

Rabbi Horowitz introduced himself. A smile broke out on Mr. Lattori's stern looking face when the Rabbi said;" This is Mr. Yakov Yakov." This of course had to be followed by the explanation of how his name came about.

This made Mr. Lattori smile even wider.

"Mr. Lattori, said the Rabbi, Mr. Yakov wants to open a chiropractic clinic." Before he could continue Mr. Lattori asked, "What's a dat ting?"

Mr. Lattori, like Yakov, was also an immigrant. He still needed help with his English. But he was constantly learning new things. "What's a dat," he asked again. The Rabbi asked Yakov, in Russian, to explain to him exactly what chiropractics was. The Rabbi had heard of it but in the rush of things he never asked Yakov exactly what it was. Yakov explained to Rabbi Horowitz and the Rabbi tried to translate what Yakov had said to Mr. Lattori.

"I no rent noting to soma body who do dat," said Mr. Lattori, waving his hands back and forth in the air. Yakov understood that gesture. He got up, walked over behind Mr. Lattori, who was walking away, and pulled him into his arms.

"What you do? What you do?" Yelled Mr. Lattori. With rapid movements Yakov was behind him, put his arms under his, and locked his hands on his chest. He lifted Mr. Lattori off his feet and curved his back at the same time. Mr. Lattori protested the whole time. A large pop was heard in the room and Yakov lowered him to his feet and released him. The Rabbi apologized profusely. Mr. Lattori's pain in his lower back that he had suffered with for months was gone. Yakov had suspected that Mr. Lattori was in pain by the way he held his right hand on his lower back. And the tentative steps when he walked confirmed it. Mr. Lattori turned his body cautiously, left than right, gyrated from the waist up, went to his desk and asked.

"What you want to rent?" The Rabbi explained where the property was and what part of the building he wanted to rent.

"You no want all factory?" Mr. Lattori asked? The Rabbi thought for a moment and replied," For now he wants only the office space." How prophetic this reply would eventually turn out to be.

"If he do me soma more, I rent," said Mr. Lattori. "But ifa I rent factory to somabody he go." The Rabbi knew that wouldn't happen any time soon. The country was in a deep recession. The government had nothing good to report.

A figure of ten dollars a month was agreed upon. And if Mr. Lattori came in for a treatment, Yakov would pay only five dollars for that month.

"You see lawyer two days. Sign papers, get key," said Mr. Lattori. He handed the Rabbi his business card with the lawyers name and address on it. He couldn't believe it had actually happened. Yakov's wife would never believe it either.

On the agreed day, Nadya, Yakov, and Rabbi Horowitz, found the lawyer's office. The law partners of the firm Higgins and O'Leary were still in disbelief that Mr. Latorri had decided to make this deal. Over the phone, Mr. Higgins had tried to talk Mr. Lattori out of it. It didn't seem to be good business to the lawyer. But He was a man of his word.

"Mr. Higgins may we have the key to the property so that we may inspect it," asked the rabbi. The key was given to Yakov and the three of them left the lawyer's office. They decided that there was enough daylight to go and inspect the property.

A light misty rain was falling as Yakov, his wife, and the Rabbi, walked the five or six blocks to the factory. Outside, the addition looked in remarkably good condition. It was raining harder now. Yakov put the key in the lock. At first it wouldn't turn from lack of use. "Let me try it?" asked the Rabbi. Back and forth he turned the key, being careful not to use too much pressure. A broken key would not get them out of the rain. Finally the lock turned. A little nudge and the sticking door opened.

The three of them stood inside by the door and gazed around the room. The two sidewalls each had three windows. The door was centered on its wall with a window on either side of the entrance. What light there was from the overcast day had trouble penetrating the grime that coated the windows. Miraculously only three windowpanes were broken. A slow but steady drip fell from the ceiling in the corner where the west wall connected to the factory wall. A heavy sliding door, secured with a large deadbolt, covered the entrance to the factory.

The plastered walls and ceiling were in desperate need of washing and painting. Four lamps, with white and green enameled reflectors, hung from the ceiling by long brass chains. Yakov turned the four switches to the left of the door. Two of the lamps lit. A simultaneous cheer echoed in the room. The glow from the lights lifted their spirits momentarily. Basically the structure inside was sound. With a few days of work and paint this was just what Yakov wanted. Nadya and the Rabbi were not as sure as Yakov was.

The lavatory and sink, partitioned in the corner opposite the roof leak, was a disaster. The water pipes came into this cubicle through the factory wall. A heavy coating of dust covered the white sink and toilet. Yakov turned the faucet handle on the sink. There was no water. The steam radiators hadn't held any water for a longtime. These pipes also came from the other side of the factory wall. For a long time no one spoke. Nadya finally asked, "What can we do?"

"You must have water and heat," said the Rabbi. "Who can do this kind of work? It will cost a lot of money," he added.

Totally depressed, they walked outside. Yakov locked the door. The rain had stopped and it was getting late. Half way back to the synagogue Nadya asked the Rabbi, "In America, isn't the owner of a building responsible for its condition?"

"I don't know, said the rabbi. This is all new to me."

Even though Nadya was in constant pain her mind was sharp. "Maybe there is something in a lease about the condition of the property," she said. They quickened their pace to get back home. With a deep sigh Yakov said," we have so much to learn." The next day the Rabbi and Yakov returned to the Higgins law firm. Mr. Higgins assigned a law clerk to answer any of their questions. He showed them a blank lease.

The lease was three pages long. It was a standard lease that had blank spaces that would be typed in with the appropriate information.

And the small print made it difficult to read. After much debate they decided that Yakov was the lessee and Mr. Lattori, the lease holder. The Rabbi began reading the neatly printed pages. After a long silence the Rabbi shouted, "Aha. Here it is." The lease holder is responsible for the water, the heating, the lighting, and the plumbing." They showed the lines in the contract to the clerk and he confirmed that they were correct.

After much discussion they decided that a visit to Mr. Lattori was in order.

Early the next morning they returned to Mr. Lattori's house. The Rabbi rang the bell. After a short wait the door slowly opened. Yakov and the Rabbi were greeted by a stunning statuesque woman.

"May I help you," she asked?

"The Rabbi responded," We would like to see Mr. Lattori."

"Mr. Lattori is not available at the moment. May I be of assistance? I'm Mrs. Lattori," she replied.

"We need to see him about a property that Mr. Yakov wants to rent from him. Yesterday we spoke to him about it. Mr. Yakov doesn't speak English very well. I am his interpreter," said the Rabbi.

"Please come in. I handle all of Mr. Lattori's business dealings. My husband told me about Mr. Yakov and his interesting encounter with Mr. Lattori," she smiled.

What Mrs. Lattori did not mention was the fact that her husband was the nephew of Don Salvatore Mancini, the mob boss of all New York City. The mob controlled drugs, prostitution, booze, trucking, and the very lucrative garbage collection business. It was widely known that Vincent Lattori was tolerated among the mobsters only because he was the Don's nephew.

It was also known through out the inner circles and to the Don himself that it was Vincent's wife, Victoria, who ran the garbage business. She had earned a business degree from New York City College. She knew garbage and her connections at City Hall liked her. It wasn't respect out of fear of the mob that made her good at what she did. She was smart and did her job very well. Her charm and good looks were an extra plus.

31

"How can I help you", she asked?

The Rabbi explained to her what they had experienced at the rental site. Apologetically he also explained that it was the owner's responsibility to provide the necessary services, according to the lease.

"I am very sorry for that and you are absolutely right. Mr. Lattori did not realize the bad condition that the building was in. I normally handle all the rentals," she said.

At that moment Mr. Lattori entered the room dressed in a loosely fitting bathrobe.

"Yakov, you do me now," he said, in a demanding voice.

"Vincent, Mr. Yakov and the Rabbi are her on business. Can you wait a few minutes and I am sure Mr. Yakov will be happy to give you a treatment," she quietly said.

"I give you treatment now if you open Goddamn mouth again," yelled Mr. Lattori. "Yakov, you do me now," he screamed.

Yakov and the Rabbi were stunned by his crude behavior. The mob boss took two steps toward his wife with his fist raised.

The Rabbi stepped in front of him.

"Stop, in the name of God," he said loudly.

Mr. Lattori stopped, uttered some Italian obscenities at them, and left.

Mrs. Lattori didn't seem too upset at her husband's behavior.

"Please accept my apology. He isn't always like that," she said quietly.

"Will you be alright," asked the Rabbi.

"Yes, thank you." Without skipping a beat, she continued. "There is an identical building a block away that is in much better condition. You can have it for the same rent. I will also put my carpenter, Leonard Travis, at your disposal. He can fix anything that needs to be done at my expense."

THE BREATH OF FREEDOM

The Rabbi explained the deal to Yakov. He nodded his approval. They thanked the gracious Mrs. Lattori.

"I will inform Mr. Higgins and he will have the key ready. Tomorrow you and the Rabbi can inspect the building at your leisure," said Mrs. Lattori. She escorted them to the door and they left.

The next morning, Nadya, Yakov, and the Rabbi, arrived at the new location. Leonard, the carpenter, greeted them and handed Yakov the key. He unlocked the door and the four of them entered the factory office room. Just as Mrs. Lattori had said, this building was in much better shape.

Yakov immediately began visualizing what he wanted to do in the office space. He picked up an old broom that lay on the floor. In the light dust that lay on the floor he began to draw the positions of the partitions with the broom handle. Leonard took a piece of paper from his pocket and sketched a rough drawing of the outline that Yakov had etched on the floor. There would be two treatment rooms. A hallway against the back wall, to the right, would lead to the enclosed lavatory in the corner. A left turn in the hallway would lead to a bedroom and a petitioned-off space that would serve as the kitchen.

Yakov instructed the Rabbi to ask Leonard if he could do it. The carpenter nodded "yes". Yakov was ecstatic; he grabbed the Rabbi and Leonard and began singing and dancing. As they twirled about the Rabbi asked Leonard when he could start. Tomorrow was translated into Russian. Yakov sang and danced louder and faster until they all dropped to the floor exhausted. The next day the work began. It would go on for three weeks.

CHAPTER 6

The Consulate

Yakov had put off his visit to the Russian consulate as long as he could. Two weeks had passed and now he had to do it. He had turned down Rabbi Horowitz's offer to go with him. This was a fear he had to face alone. The letter that he was to send back to Moscow was in his jacket pocket. His father had set it up this way. Once the letter reached the Kremlin, Gerog, his beloved father, would turn over the journal to the pedophile Brezhinski. Giving him the book would eventually lead to Gerog's death. Yakov was sure of this. His mother would also pay in other ways for helping him and his family to escape. Yakov vowed that he would spend his life helping those who yearned for freedom, just as the rabbi and his wife had done. Yakov and Nadya could never repay them for all that they had done for them.

Even after two weeks in America Yakov still did not have that deep, down in his bones feeling that he was free. At times it felt like a dream and he would awaken to find that they were still in Russia. These thoughts were probably caused by the physical effort that it was taking to adapt to a society that was so different from what they had left.

Communism was kept alive by the absolute power that only those few men at the top of the party wielded. They gave themselves the best food, fine homes, acquired stashes of money, and an endless supply of vodka and cigarettes. The blood and suffering of the oppressed millions of Russians and non-Russians alike seldom entered their Communist conscience. Those at the top were only mainly concerned with just two goals: how to keep the power they had, and how to increase that power if they could. Every one of them knew that the more power you had increased your longevity. Yakov knew that his father, was one of the few men in the Kremlin with a conscience and also knew that he had helped give birth to this political horror. From the lowliest peasant to Stalin himself, no one was safe. His father probably thought his death would be partial atonement for the part he had played in keeping the beast alive.

Yakov stood in front of the Russian Consulate for a long time.

The drab, gray sandstone building was not an inviting architectural marvel. All the windows facing the street had closed heavy blinds on them. Steel bars stretched across every window, front, back, and sides. Two Russian soldiers with loaded rifles guarded the entrance. A large sign written in Russian and English said, "Halt. The guard will escort you inside."

Yakov trembled as he stood at the bottom of the stairs. Rabbi Horowitz had told Yakov the rumors about Russians going into the consulate and never coming out again. But he said he personally didn't know of anyone that it had happened to. The thought raced in his mind. The anxiety within him was overwhelming. He paced back and forth.

Yakov had a piece of paper in his shirt pocket. His name and the address of his new home were written on it. He also had the letter that he was to send back to Russia for his father.

A New York City patrolman, Arnie Langston, stood on the sidewalk at the edge of the consulate property. By international law he was not allowed to stand on consulate property. He

35

was there to make sure demonstrators understood the law. Demonstrating on the sidewalk in front of the consulate was, by law, trespassing. Doing it in the street, in a peaceful manner, was O.K., only as long as traffic was not impeded. It was a discretionary thing depending on the officer who was on duty.

Yakov's heart was beating rapidly. He approached the officer. In Russia he would not have dared to speak to a policeman. There they were part of the corruption that infected everything in life. Yakov partially overcame his fear. With the paper in his hand he pointed at his name and slowly said," My name is Yakov Yakov. I go." He stopped and pointed to the consulate, then at the officer, and then pointed at the ground twice.

"What are you trying to say? I don't understand," responded Officer Arnie Langston. Are you afraid of something?'

"Da da, Yakov translated, yes, yes."

"Why are you afraid?' The officer managed to get the idea across through gestures.

Yakov pointed to himself. Then he turned and took three steps toward the Russian Consulate. He turned and faced the officer, placed his index finger to his temple, and then fell to the ground as if he had been shot. Officer Langston smiled as he helped Yakov to his feet. "No. No. No.," he said. "This is America. No one will harm you here. Wait! He waved his hands in front of him, walked over to a lamppost, crossed his arms and leaned against it. He pointed to his eyes, then to the consulate. "I," pointing to himself, "will wait here," pointing to the ground where he stood. Yakov understood. He gave the officer a weak smile and nodded his head. The policeman put his arm over Yakov's shoulder, walked him to the bottom step, and nudged him forward. Yakov walked up the steps. He turned and gave him another thin smile, walked to the top of the steps, spoke to the guard, and they entered the building.

The guard took Yakov to the receptionist seated behind a large desk. He showed her the three diplomatic visas. She was dressed in the female version of a military uniform. Her hair was rolled into a tight bun. There was no expression on her face as she looked at the documents.

"Where are your wife and child?" she asked.

"They are staying with a friend. My son developed a fever last night and we thought it best that they stay at home," said Yakov. It was only a little lie.

"Whom do you wish to see," she asked.

"I wish to report to the minister in charge of the consulate," Said Yakov.

"Be seated. I will tell him you are here," she said. Taking the visas with her she entered the door behind her desk. Several minutes passed. The door opened and she returned to her desk.

"Minister Petroff will see you now," she announced.

"Comrade Yakov, it is good to see you. I know your father. I hope he is well." Said minister Petroff.

"Thank you minister. My mother and father are both well," replied Yakov.

"I see by your diplomatic visas that you are on a fact finding mission. You should have come here as soon as you were settled. We could have helped you," said Petroff.

"I humbly beg your patience Minister Petroff. My wife Nadya became ill three days after we arrived. She has finally recovered enough that I could leave her to come here," replied Yakov.

"Where have you been staying," asked the minister. Yakov was stunned by the question. He did not want to mention the Rabbi. He pictured Rabbi Horowitz and his wife dead on the synagogue floor. Yakov was beginning to sweat. He took the paper with his address on it and handed it to Minister Petroff. The minister wrote it down and handed it back to Yakov

"It says on your visa that you and your wife are on a fact-finding mission of the medical system in America," said the minister. Yakov suddenly remembered something the minister had said. He knew his father in Moscow.

Yakov took a deep breath and said," My father has been keeping a journal about many of his old friends that were with him in the glorious revolution." The minister's face paled. His demeanor suddenly changed.

"Did he mention if my name was in it? Why is he keeping a journal? What is he going to do with it?" He almost screamed the last question. The secretary came to the door and asked if everything was alright.

"Da, Da," he replied in a quieter tone.

Yakov answered the last question. "He is going to write a book about our greatest triumph, the Russian revolution. It will be more monumental than Lenin's writings."

Yakov had played his ace and it worked. Another little lie and he escaped telling the Minister about the Rabbi. He did not want to reveal his name to the Minister.

"Minister Petroff, I have this letter addressed to Comrade Brezhinski, the minister of foreign travel. It has some of our research on American medicine that must go out with the next courier leaving for Moscow," said Yakov.

Minister Petroff's hand slightly shook as he took the letter

"There is a courier leaving in the morning. I will see to it that it is in his case," said the minister.

"Respectfully I thank you sir. I will tell my father that I met you when I write to him tomorrow. I will mention your kindness to me," replied Yakov.

Yakov literally burst through the front door. The guard nearly leveled his rifle at him. He ran down the stairs. In four

THE BREATH OF FREEDOM

leaps he reached the officer, kissed him on both cheeks and rambled on in Russian telling him all that had transpired. When he got to the part about the letter he suddenly froze. Endless tears streamed down his face. He slumped to the sidewalk and sobbed. The officer was totally bewildered.

"Can I walk you home," asked the officer? With a few gestures Yakov understood him. Yakov handed Officer Langston the piece of paper with his address on it. He took the paper from Yakov, stood him up, and walked him home. When they got there the Rabbi and Nadya were waiting. Nadya took Yakov and put him to bed. Rabbi Horowitz introduced himself to the officer and explained Yakov's visit to the consulate. When he finished telling him about the letter and what it meant to Yakov they both had tears running down their faces.

CHAPTER 9

THE LETTER

It took seventeen days for the letter to reach Comrade Brezhinski's desk. He notified Gerog Yakov by phone that the letter had arrived. An appointment was made for the following day at 2:00 PM. Gerog was too upset to finish the day. He told his secretary that he was taking the rest of the day off. Gerog also informed her that he had an important meeting tomorrow with Comrade Brezhinski and he wouldn't be coming in.

Gerog's secretary was an attractive bright girl in her mid twenties. Her father had been an officer in the Russian navy. One day he disappeared. The official report listed him and his ship's crew as lost at sea. Gerog, from his numerous connections, had learned that he was suspected of plotting to kill Stalin. There was no evidence of that but the suspicion was enough to consider him a threat. He simply disappeared.

Gerog Yakov, endangering himself, told his secretary the truth. He made her promise never to say a word. She and her mother were eternally grateful to Gerog. Occasionally Gerog and his wife would have them over for dinner. Gerog was always giving the girl a few extra rubles. His salary was much more than he and his wife needed. It made Gerog feel good helping her and her mother. They had so little.

THE BREATH OF FREEDOM

Gerog was up early the next day. His wife had also risen early. As she fixed a light breakfast they discussed what he was going to say to Brezhinski. After eating he went to the market to see if any meat was available. Most of it would be sold in an hour. When he got there a small line was already forming. While Gerog waited he folded up several rubles and held them in the palm of his hand. When he got to the counter he shook hands with the butcher and the rubles were exchanged. The butcher went into the back room and returned with a package. Gerog took the package and left. He hated bribing the butcher but he wanted to have something special for his secretary and her mother when they came to supper that evening. He took the meat home before he went to his appointment.

It seemed like an eternity to Gerog but the appointed hour finally arrived. He walked into Brezhinski's outer office and greeted his secretary. The door to his office was closed. She advised Gerog, "At the moment the minister's wife is with him."

He sat down and waited. By his watch thirty-two minutes had passed. He could not stand the waiting. Gerog got up, walked over to the heavy oak door. He was about to knock when he heard her voice.

"The monster is dead. The monster is dead," she repeated over and over. Slowly Gerog opened the door. Lying on the floor, covered in blood, was the minister's wife. Still seated in his desk chair the minister was slumped forward, laying on his chest, in a pool of blood. His head rested on its left side. The eyes were open. Gerog could see the opening beneath his chin.

"Gerog shouted," Call the captain of the guards. Call them now." The secretary ran to the office door, let out a scream, and fainted.

"I have saved the children of Moscow. I have saved them all. I killed the monster," yelled Mrs. Brezhinski. Gerog grabbed the phone on the desk. He felt the warm blood on it.

41

"Send the captain of the guard immediately to Minister Brezhinski's office. There has been a murder," Gerog yelled into the receiver.

While Gerog stood behind the desk he glanced up and saw the journal. He reached up, removed it from the shelf, and stuck it into his inner coat pocket. A second later Captain Uri Sukov arrived. His men took the secretary and laid her on a couch in the outer office. Slowly the captain stepped into the crime scene, walked to his left and looked at the minister's wife. She was now mumbling incoherently still lying on the floor. He walked around her and approached the body being careful not to step in any blood.

Stopping next to Gerog he asked," Who are you?"

"I am Minister Gerog Yakov, he replied. I am the one who called you after the secretary fainted."

"Why are you here," asked Captain Sukov.

"I had an appointment with the minister for 2:0'clock. After waiting thirty-two minutes I approached the door and heard his wife yelling. I opened the door and this is what I found," explained Yakov.

"How did you get the blood on your right hand," asked the officer.

"I must have gotten it from the phone. It had blood on it when I used it to call you," said Yakov.

"Did you move the murder weapon," asked the captain?

"No. I didn't touch anything except the phone," lied Yakov. This lie was much bigger. The captain of the guard called one of his men.

"Search the room for a weapon," he ordered. No weapon was found. The captain asked Gerog to go sit in a chair at the far corner of the room. The officer slowly walked around the room avoiding the blood areas. He stepped over to Mrs. Brezhinski who was now lying quietly. He noticed her right hand was covered by a portion of her skirt. Her left hand was visible. Slowly he lifted the material from her covered hand. The open shaving razor and her hand were drenched in blood. The Captain ordered one of his men to take the razor from the minister's wife.

As he attempted to reach for the razor she raised up on to her knees and screamed," I am the savior of Moscow's children. I have killed the evil monster." Her face was twisted grotesquely. Her eyes were the eyes of the demon that possessed her mind. She lunged at the soldier with her razor and opened a long gash in his arm. At the same moment the captain put his boot into her back and sent her sprawling across the floor, she in one direction, the razor in another. Other soldiers came in and quickly subdued her but it took three of them to do it. The captain ordered the wounded soldier to leave and see the doctor stationed in the soldier's barracks.

"Comrade Yakov, it looks pretty much like an open and shut case.

Do you have any idea what she was raving about," asked the captain?

Yakov replied with another lie," No captain. It seemed to me like the ravings of a mad woman."

"It made no sense to me either. We'll remove her and her husband and send someone in to clean the place up. We'll need a signed statement from you stating your involvement in the proceedings. Tomorrow will be soon enough," said the captain.

Gerog was not sad that Brezhinski was dead. It was ironic that it had happened when it did. A death sentence had been lifted from Gerog's future. He saw the blood covered letter on the desk from America. He was sure it was the letter that he had given Yakov. The letter had arrived but Gerog did not try to remove it. Brezhinski's blood would have shown the outline of the removed letter. He knew the children were safe in America without seeing the content of the letter.

43

That evening, Gerog, in spite of the tragic day's events, was in a jovial mood. His wife had prepared a wonderful pot roast from the meat he had purchased. He did not spoil the evening by relating to his wife and guests what had happened in Minister Brezhinski's office.

The next morning Gerog went to work. His secretary was already at her desk. As he was about to enter his office she spoke to him.

"Minister Yakov, the gossip about Minister Brezhinski is everywhere. They are saying that you were there when it happened," she said.

"It's true. It was a ghastly sight. I wish I had been able to stop her," he replied.

"Why didn't you tell us last night," she asked?

"I didn't want to spoil the evening with such terrible talk," he replied.

"You're right, Sir. Mother would have been very upset over it. Thank you for that. She enjoyed the night so much," she said.

"Excuse me. I must prepare a report for the Captain of the Guard, Sukov. He asked me to bring it by today," he said. Gerog entered his office and closed the door.

When Gerog had finished his notes he took them to his secretary for typing. When she was done she put the pages in a large envelope. He wasn't sure where the captain's office was or if he was in. Gerog asked her to phone him. She told him he was there and where his office was.

The office was down in the basement of the building. He entered a large room. Several wooden chairs were scattered around a heavy table. Six soldiers occupied some of the chairs. Their rifles were in a rack standing next to a closed door. Gerog asked where the captain was. One of the soldiers got up, walked to the door, and knocked. A voice inside said enter. He opened it and gestured to Gerog to go in. As he walked in

44

THE BREATH OF FREEDOM

The captain jumped to his feet, walked over to Gerog, and vigorously shook his hand.

"Welcome comrade, welcome. Be seated. It's good to see you again," he said.

The captain's smile and his warm greeting made Gerog uneasy.

"I have the report that you asked for, Captain. The captain did not open the envelope and set it aside.

"I tried not to leave anything out. It was a horrible crime," said Gerog.

"Yes. Yes it was. But some new information has come up. Maybe you can help me clear up some points," asked the captain.

"I think I have given you everything that I know in my report," said Gerog. He tried to remain calm.

"Something in Mrs. Brezhnev's ranting bothered me. At the hospital she was given a shot to calm her. I gently asked her what she had meant when she spoke of the boys of Moscow. She started to become agitated again. I quietly calmed her and she explained that Brezhnev was using derelict boys for sex purposes. She said that he was evil and had to be destroyed. The dead boy in the woods told her he must die. The captain was no longer smiling. Did you know he was a pedophile?", he quietly asked.

Gerog chose his words carefully.

"Yes, I did," he said softly.

"We found the boy's body early this morning. Scavengers had eaten most of it. Did you know about the boy?", asked the captain.

Gerog realized that only the truth might save him now. Once again the specter of his death entered his mind. But he had no other choice. He was going to put his trust in the hands of the captain.

45

"I found out about Brezhinski's perversion three months ago. He had sent a car for me. The driver said he was to take me immediately to his home. It was in the middle of the night. I got dressed and went with the driver. The car stopped at the gate. I got out and the car left. I rang the bell. No one answered. I pounded on the door loudly. When Brezhinski finally answered the door he was visibly upset. We hurriedly went up the stairs to his room. I was horrified at what I saw. Lying on the floor, in a pool of blood, was the body of a young boy. He couldn't have been much more than twelve. Brezhnev kept muttering, "help me, help me. This will ruin me."

"How was the boy killed?", asked the Captain.

"I can only surmise what had happened. I have no medical training. Lying on the bed, covered with blood, was a wooden object shaped like a large penis. While in a drunken sexual frenzy, Minister Brezhinski apparently had tried to use it on the small boy and ruptured his colon. Two empty bottles of vodka were on the floor near the bed," Yakov painfully related the scene.

"Was it you who Mrs. Brezhinski saw burying the boy?", the captain whispered.

In a quiet voice Yakov responded, "Yes, it was me. I knew that if I had refused to help him, in a matter of days, I would have disappeared, along with all of my family. It would have been like we had never existed."

The captain believed Gerog. As in many other cases that he had investigated witnesses suddenly would vanish. Many of the Captain's cases could never be solved.

"Thank you Gerog. You have been very cooperative. I will mention that in my final report," said Captain Sukov.

In a trembling voice Gerog asked, "Will I be going to prison"?

"I don't know the answer to that question yet. Let me tell you about the second item that is confusing me. How you

THE BREATH OF FREEDOM

answer will give me a clearer picture about your future," said the Captain.

Yakov replied," I promise, on my mother's grave, I will give you only the truth."

The captain continued, "That evening, after the blood in the office had been cleaned up, I returned to the crime scene. While I was standing in the doorway to the office I slowly scanned the room. Something directly behind the minister's desk caught my eye. There were several book shelves with every shelf neatly filled with books from side to side."

Yakov's heart was pounding in his chest. He knew where this was leading.

"Captain, I need to tell you a story," said Gerog.

"I'm sure you do," he replied.

Gerog told him everything beginning with the growing disenchantment that had taken over his very soul. He explained carefully how he wanted his children to be free. Then he told him how he had used his journal to force Brezhinski into giving him the visas for his children.

"The space that you saw on the top shelf was where I had safely hidden the journal. I was going to give the minister the journal the day that he was murdered. When I saw what had happened I retrieved the book," said Yakov.

When Gerog had finished the captain sat in stunned silence. He could not believe what he had heard. This man was willing to give up his life for his family. He admired his courage.

He cleared his throat and finally spoke, "Where is the journal now?"

"I have it in my coat pocket," said Gerog. With all that had transpired he had forgotten to remove it from his coat. He took it out and handed it to the Captain. As he began to read it, he stopped. He walked to the door, opened it and checked on his men. He then ordered them to go and inspect

47

various parts of the building. Closing the door he returned to his desk.

Like Gerog he did not smoke and only on occasion did he drink. This was one of those times. He took a bottle of vodka and a glass from the bottom drawer of his desk. He poured one drink and returned the bottle to the desk drawer. He read more pages as he sipped the drink. He stopped, closed the book and spoke.

He pulled his chair closer to Gerog and almost in a whisper he asked, "Who else knows of this journal."

Gerog was surprised by the question. He answered,

"Only my son in America knows."

Jumping to his feet he began shaking Gerog's hand.

In a loud voice he said, "Thank you for coming in Mr. Yakov. You have cleared up all of my questions. If there is anything new to report I will call you. You are free to go. My report will state that you cooperated completely and the case is officially closed." He again leaned over and quietly said, "You must never speak of the journal to anyone ever again. It could destroy us both. Remember that." Completely stunned, Gerog left the office and went home.

Three weeks passed. On the Monday of the fourth week Gerog went to work as usual. When he arrived at his office workmen were busy removing packed boxes and furniture. His secretary was smiling. She shook his hand wildly.

"What is going on here," he asked stunned?

"Haven't they told you? You have been promoted. You are the new minister of travel. We are moving into Minister Brezhinski's old office," she squealed. Gerog wondered why he hadn't been informed of the promotion.

Speechless, he collapsed onto the only chair left in the room. Just then the Captain of the Guard walked in.

"Congratulations, he said. I couldn't wait to see you and tell you how excited I was about your promotion. I just found out about it yesterday."

Yakov noticed the new uniform the captain was wearing and the shinny pins that denoted the rank of major attached to his jacket collar.

A smile crossed Yakov's face. He now understood what had transpired. "Thank you Major for all your kindness, and congratulations on your promotion," he said.

. "Some events do have happy endings," said the major.

They shook hands warmly. Major Sukov turned and left. For Gerog it was the first time in many years that he felt that there was someone he could trust.

Gerog threw himself into his new job. He knew nothing concerning the ins and outs of visas, passports, or any of the legal aspects involved. He asked Brezhinski's secretary if she would be interested in staying and working for him. The way her face lit up said it all. He notified the two women that they could work out the details of running the office. Any changes they wished to make would be discussed with him. Suggestions would be welcome. In less than a week the office was running efficiently. Gerog was so grateful for the women and how they had taken control, he gave them each a raise.

As things settled down and routines established, Gerog finally had time to write a long letter to his son. He did not dare write any details about what had transpired. Mail was often secretly opened. Brezhinski's death he omitted entirely. He mentioned his promotion and said that he hoped to spend many years at his new job. That was the closest he dared to come in telling Yakov that the eminent threat of his death from the journal was gone. The next day the letter left with a courier bound for the Russian consulate in New York City.

The courier got there in eighteen days. The Russian propaganda constantly told the Russian people how morally corrupt America was. But Russian diplomats loved going to New York, and shopping was high on their list of things to do. Most of the luggage that they brought to America was nearly empty. On the journey home those same bags were bursting at the seams. And for some strange reason connections to America were always easier to make. Going home often took 12 to 14 days.

The phone call from the Russian consulate came as a surprise to Yakov and Nadya. The Rabbi's wife had taken the call. She was concerned that the consulate had their number and she wondered how they had gotten it.

"Yes, she said, I will give the Yakov's the message that they have a diplomatic letter waiting for them at the consulate. Thank you."

Upon their return to the synagogue later that day Mrs. Horowitz immediately gave the news to the Yakov's. Yakov was sure it was about his father and that the news was bad. Yakov, Nadya, and the Rabbi hurried to the consulate.

They arrived just as the consulate was closing for the day.

Minister Petroff had heard their excited arrival and was waiting at his office door with the letter in his hand.

"It is from your father," said the minister. He handed Yakov the letter. Yakov was afraid to open it. Slowly his trembling fingers tore open the seal and he began to read it. When he got to the line about his father's promotion and how he planned to spend many years at his new job Yakov embraced Nadya.

"He is safe and well", he whispered to her. This news was overwhelming. He handed the letter to the Rabbi. He read it aloud and joined them in their embrace. Yakov could not imagine how he had managed to survive.

CHAPTER 10

THE PRACTICE

Sometimes the casual meeting of totally unrelated people can produce a scenario that is so unreal that it has no logical explanation. It began with the arrival of Mrs. Victoria Lattori at the factory office site to see what progress had been made on the remodeling. That day Rabbi Horowitz had also come for a look-see.

As she stepped into the building she called to the Rabbi.

"Rabbi have you seen Mr. Yakov and his wife", she asked.

"Nadya is at the synagogue and Yakov is speaking to Leonard at he far end of the office", he replied.

"Would you get him? I need to speak to him and I will need you to interpret," she requested.

A few moments later he returned with Yakov. Mrs. Lattori quickly got to the point of her visit.

"Mr. Yakov, before you can open your office you will need to obtain a city license to operate your business. Go to City Hall tomorrow and get one." She ended her visit by asking Yakov about Nadya's health. He replied that she was feeling better. She turned and left.

The Rabbi slowly repeated to Yakov what she had said. Early the next day Yakov and the Rabbi boarded the downtown bus. After traveling several stops they asked for transfers, got off, and waited for a few minutes. They used their transfer tickets and boarded the Hudson Street bus.

Thirty-two blocks later they arrived at Duane Street, got off the bus, and walked the block and a half to City Hall. The building looked even more ominous than it did the day they went to the Maps and Plats office.

They entered the main door. Inside the lobby they walked over to the information desk. The Rabbi asked the young lady behind the counter," Where is the license bureau?"

"Father, which license bureau do you want? We have marriage, drivers, garbage, commercial, and several other licenses I can't pronounce," she responded.

The Rabbi corrected her," I'm not a priest. I'm a Rabbi. I think it's a commercial license that we need."

"I'm sorry Rabbi. I should have known when I saw your beard. Commercial licenses are available on the third floor, room 312," she responded.

Room 312 had no windows. It was a lot cleaner than the maps and plats office, but darker. Behind the counter at her desk sat a middle aged frumpy-looking woman. Her glasses were pushed up on her forehead. She sat in a chair behind her desk facing the counter; her head was tilted slightly to the right. When she needed to turn her head she would swivel the chair to the right or left to change her line of sight. This was the way she controlled the excruciating pain in her neck.

"What can I do for you?" she asked.

"My friend does not speak English. Mr. Yakov Yakov has a degree from the Moscow Institute of Chiropractic. He wants to open an office here in New York," said the Rabbi. Gertrude, the clerk, turned her chair to the right to look at Yakov and then turned it to the left to look at the Rabbi. After a long silence, as she was trying hard to keep from laughing so as not to feel the pain, she responded.

THE BREATH OF FREEDOM

"Is this some kind of a joke? He speaks no English and . . ."

"We practice every night and he is learning very fast. Just listen. Yakov what is your name? The Rabbi asked slowly."

Yakov responded in Russian.

"No, no, Yakov. English, say it in English," pleaded the Rabbi.

"Oh, oh. Yes. My name is Yakov Yakov," he carefully replied.

"What's with the two names?" She asked, almost smiling.

"Madam please let that go. It is his real name and it is a very long story," begged the Rabbi.

Yakov was getting impatient and asked Rabbi Horowitz, in Russian, what was taking so long. He explained to Yakov, as best he could, what the delay was. Yakov studied Gertrude carefully as she spoke again.

"Everything else aside, the name, the lack of English, the biggest problem he faces is that he did not graduate from an American school. He cannot practice his trade without an American degree. That's the law," she said as she threw her hands up above her head and waved them from side to side. English or no English Yakov had already demonstrated that he knew what the gesture meant.

Yakov walked to the end of the counter and crossed the yellow painted words that said "do not cross".

Gertrude protested vehemently, "Get back. Get back behind the line," she yelled as she stood up.

Yakov moved like a leopard. Swiftly he spun her around, slipped his arms under her arms and placed his right hand on her chest. With his left hand he grabbed her chin and gave her head a quick twist to the left. With one motion Yakov was able to completely stop the pain that had plagued Gertrude for weeks. She stood there absolutely stunned. Her glasses came to rest on her nose slightly askew. She painlessly

53

turned her head, looked at the Rabbi, and asked," How did he do that"?

"I don't know, said the Rabbi, but that's what he does."

She sat down, opened the top drawer of her desk, took out the application and handed it to the Rabbi.

"Fill this out and when you get to the line where it asks for the name of the school, write down "The Moscow School of Chiropractic, New York City Campus." Gertrude and the Rabbi laughed loudly. Yakov didn't need any translation. Yakov hugged her and kissed her on both cheeks in the European custom. Yakov took both of her hands in his, looked into her eyes, and in perfect English he said," Thank you."

"No, no, she said. It is I who thank you. Welcome to America. And good luck in your work."

Yakov and the Rabbi talked and laughed all the way down to the street.

"Freedom, freedom, sweet freedom, said Yakov. Breathe deeply Rabbi. You can smell it in the air."

He unfolded the license, touched the raised letters of the notary seal, and kissed the paper. The Northbound bus carried the jubilant pair home.

They burst through the door yelling and jumping while holding the license in the air. The women joined in the celebration.

"Yakov, I have a surprise for you," shouted Nadya. She pulled Yakov by the hand over to the table. The handed painted sign on the table said. "Dr. Yakov Yakov, Chiropractor."

As the four of them looked at the sign, Yakov could no longer hold back the tears. They hugged and kissed and hugged some more. His father's dream of freedom for his children was coming true.

There had been some delays in the remodeling of the factory office. Leonard had tried very hard to complete it within the three-week period. Again there had been a problem with getting the right permits. Gertrude Larson was asked by Yakov and the Rabbi if she could help with the paperwork. She told them that filling out the papers was not the problem. The delay was caused by arranging for the bribes. Certain people in the building trades had to be paid off. It took time to find which of the building trades were involved. Who was to receive the money, how much, and where the cash was to be delivered had to be worked out. Two people were to get twenty dollars apiece. Gertrude, who was now getting weekly chiropractic adjustments from Yakov, negotiated the deal.

At the end of the fourth week the work was completed. Nadya had asked Leonard to hang the sign she had painted on the outside wall next to the entrance. The next day two patients had come to the office. Gertrude and Mrs. Lattori had recommended to them to try Yakov's practice. By the end of the week Yakov had seen five patients.

Yakov and Nadya were thrilled that a little money from Yakov's work was coming in. He still had a large portion of the American money that his father had given him. Rabbi Horowitz had exchanged Yakov's Russian rubles for dollars. Yakov had given them to the Rabbi for all the help that this good man had given to Nadya and him. It didn't amount to much as the exchange rate was very low.

Yakov's first patients were some of the earliest people that he and the Rabbi had met. Mr. Lattori had already been in twice for treatments. Mrs. Lattori came in for the first time complaining about a pain in her lower back. Dr. Yakov noticed that she had a bruise in that area.

"How did you get this bruise," he asked?

"I tripped over a rug. And when I fell I hit my back on the corner of the table," she replied.

Yakov was suspicious about the bruise but did not pursue the matter. The good news was that according to their lease agreement each time they came in five dollars was deducted from the rent. That made this month rent-free. Also Mrs. Lattori would slip Nadya an extra buck. Being a business woman she knew the Yakovs needed the money.

Gertrude, the license clerk, still needed a little more work on her neck. Yakov refused to accept money from her. He was constantly pushing his fee back into her hand. He owed so much to this kind lady. The act turned into a charade. Margaret would give up trying to pay him. But on the way out Nadya would hold out her hand, and the dollar ended up in the till.

Patrolman Arnie Langston showed up at the office two weeks after their encounter at the consulate. Again Yakov refused to take any money. Arnie had twisted his knee while trying to control a demonstration in front of The Russian Consulate. This time, as the dollar fee was pushed back and forth, Nadya simply reached over Arnie's shoulder and took the money from his hand. Arnie was so grateful for the care Yakov had given him that three days later he showed up with two of his buddies.

On Sunday, like many other businesses, the office was closed.

With no advertising and only by referrals the practice began to grow. One day an Italian woman stood outside the office door. She was in so much pain that she couldn't open it.

"Oh my God," she screamed in Italian, over and over. Nadya helped her inside. The woman was holding her right arm with her left hand. There was no blood, and nothing seemed broken. Nadya suspected that she had a dislocated shoulder. Yakov, who had been talking with the Rabbi, came over to them. Nadya placed her hands on the woman's shoulders. She pushed down until the woman figured out what Nadya was trying to do. She laid the woman on the floor. She told Yakov and the Rabbi to hold her down. Nadya sat on the floor, put her foot under her arm, and with a firm pull and a twisting action popped the shoulder back in place. They got the woman on her feet and Nadya made her a sling from a pillow case. The Italian woman bolted from the office.

"Garaci, graci, graci," she yelled as she ran down the street. An hour later she returned. With tears streaming down her face she handed Nadya a large bag. She opened it and pulled out a dressed chicken and a dozen eggs. In the building where she lived the woman raised laying chickens on the roof. The chicken in the bag had stopped laying. Nadya and Yakov were grateful for the gift. The two of them gently hugged her and thanked her for what she had done.

"This could never have happened in Russia," he whispered in Nadya's ear.

Some mornings, on the door step, there would be eggs and occasionally a chicken.

With each passing week the practice grew. But just as often as not patients that had no money would barter for their treatment. Leonard could always find something to fix when a plumber, electrician, or painter who couldn't pay was treated. It was an arrangement that would prove to be mutually beneficial when it became obvious that Yakov needed more treatment rooms. Leonard began expanding construction into the factory itself. By now Leonard had become Yakov's personal carpenter and all-around handy man. Mrs. Lattori was happy to let Leonard stay as long as Yakov needed him.

Nadya also had started to see patients. Sometimes Yakov would notice something unusual about an individual that he was treating. Even though Nadya could not practice medicine Yakov would ask her to take a look. The pain that she lived with every day had not diminished her skills as a physician. There was never any charge for what she did. And if she felt that it was something serious she would ask the patient to see a doctor.

The practice was increasing almost weekly. It was time to consider building more examination rooms inside the factory.

Mrs. Lattori had not been informed yet that they needed more rooms. It would also mean negotiating a new rental agreement.

"Yakov, said Nadya, why don't we ask Mrs. Lattori to look inside the factory."

On her next visit, after Yakov had finished treating her, he asked if they could take a look into the factory portion of the building.

"Why do you want to go in there? They used to make expensive cigars here and it still reeks of tobacco," she said.

Nadya explained," Yakov's practice is growing so fast that we need more examination rooms."

"I have other places that you could rent, larger places, nicer places," she said.

"But the people who come here know this is where we are. We might lose some of them if we moved," responded Yakov.

Just then Leonard came into the office. Yakov asked him if he had a few minutes to spare.

"Anything for you, Doc," he replied.

"Come, come," said Yakov as he led him across the room to where Mrs. Lattori stood. Leonard had not seen her when he walked in.

The shock of seeing her confused him.

"Hello, Mrs. Lattori. Am I going back to work for you? I have just started the drawings for Doctor Yakov's next project and I have a lot to do," he said.

"Leonard, it's ok. You're not going anywhere. We want to go into the factory and look around. Open the door for us," said Mrs. Lattori

Leonard unhooked the large latch on the sliding door to the abandoned factory. The four of them stepped inside. The pungent almost overpowering smell of tobacco filled the air.

"Dr. Yakov wants to build more treatment rooms in here," said Nadya. Leonard grew excited. He liked working for the Yakovs. He did not want to leave. Mrs. Lattori payed him well but this project consumed him.

"Look at the available space. The room is about 250 feet long by 70 feet wide. Two rows of steel I beams, equally spaced, hold up the second floor. The ceiling is about twelve feet high. The windows are nicely spaced so that almost all of the rooms would have a window." He began walking around stomping on the floor as he went.

"The floor is solid and more lights won't be a problem. We will need to add more radiators to increase the heat. I don't see any problems except for the addition of another lavatory some where," said Leonard.

He was so excited that he almost forgot to breathe

Mrs. Lattori said," Calm down Leonard. You will be staying here for now."

"Wait," said Yakov. He turned to Nadya and asked, "How can we pay for this? We can't ask Leonard to work for nothing. We will need materials."

Even though Yakov and Nadya spoke in Russian Mrs. Lattori pretty much guessed what they were saying.

"Nadya, tell Yakov that I would be willing to invest in your business for a five percent interest of the profits. As a business partner I will pay for the materials and Leonard's wages. When you feel that you can afford it you can buy me out."

When Nadya had finished explaining her proposition to Yakov he kissed Mrs. Lattori on both cheeks, wrapped his arms around her waist, and danced her around the room. As they whirled past Leonard she asked, "When can you get started?"

59

As they passed again, he yelled," I can start tomorrow,"

Early the next day Leonard began laying out the room locations on a drawing board. Leonard had brought his two young sons to help with the work. His sons were busy removing the special tables that tobacco workers used for rolling cigars. Stacking them outside, in front of the office, Leonard placed a for sale sign on them. By noon, at two dollars each, the twenty-three tables were soon gone. Mrs. Lattori suggested they use the money for materials.

There were hundreds of finely-made wooden cigar boxes stored in the corner of the factory. The lavish boxes complimented the fine cigars that would be housed inside. These boxes were sold for twenty cents each.

On the second floor hundreds of pounds of tobacco leaves hung on racks suspended from the ceiling. They had dried to the point that they were as brittle as autumn leaves. They were added to the other useless debris in piles and cans to be picked up on garbage day.

"Mr. Yakov, on garbage day you must hand the garbage man an envelope with five dollars in it," said Leonard.

"Why," asked Yakov?

"It would be better if Mrs. Lattori told you," replied Leonard.

"What does she have to do with our garbage," asked Nadya?

"It's not her. It's Mr. Lattori, said Leonard. But for her sake don't say anything to him."

"Leonard, does everyone in New York City have to pay?" asked Nayda.

"Yes. Please don't ask me anymore. Just pay the money. It's very dangerous if you don't," said Leonard.

Nadya carefully explained what was said to Yakov.

THE BREATH OF FREEDOM

"It is no different here than in Russia," said Yakov. Nadya translated what Yakov had said for Leonard.

"Yes it is different here. It is. Here you have your own business. Let them have the garbage. America is not perfect, but it's better than anywhere else," said Leonard.

Yakov embraced Leonard and said, "I must never forget where I came from. Thank you my friend."

CHAPTER 11

A GREAT FIND

Leonard's work was going well. Mr. Lattori had taken a personal interest in the construction. Scheduling extra visits was his way of nosing around. He couldn't figure out how easily Yakov obtained the permits for the renovation.

With her connections at city hall Gertrude was able to bypass much of the red tape, but the bribes that permeated the building trades had to be paid. Like Yakov's father she knew where a lot of the skeletons were buried.

The end of October was nearing. And New York nights were getting chilly. Leonard was ready to install three more radiators in the factory. After that he would need to fire up the boiler and check the system for leaks. Leonard's talents extended into several of the building trades. This work required a permit from the boilermaker's union. The head of the union was a tough Irishman. Leonard was unable to meet the rules that the fat mick demanded. The high cost of the permit was just a hidden bribe. Leonard told Yakov of the problem and Yakov told Gertrude. She had often served as a go-between for the married union boss and his two mistresses. The next day the permit arrived. Leonard was in shock but never asked any questions.

THE BREATH OF FREEDOM

During Yakov's training at the Moscow Chiropractic Institute he was introduced to the electronic muscle stimulator. In chiropracty this was an invaluable tool. Electrodes were taped to a muscle. A pulsating electric charge would cause the muscle to contract and relax. A timer would determine the length of the treatment and a knob controlled the intensity of the charge. The patient would tell the doctor how high a charge he or she could take. The stimulator reduced the number of treatments that were needed to help a patient to recover. It was truly a remarkable tool. Yakov dreamed of some day owning one.

After their usual Sunday dinner with Rabbi Horowitz and his wife, Yakov and the Rabbi went for a walk. During the walking and talking they had lost track of time and direction. They found themselves in an area of retail stores and several pawnshops. Window-shopping was something they had come to enjoy. As they walked past the window of a pawnshop Yakov suddenly stopped. Without turning around he walked backwards and returned to the pawnshop window. Among all the clutter in the window he spotted a black box smaller than the doctor's medical bag that was next to it.

"Yakov, what are you starring at," asked the Rabbi? Yakov could not believe his eyes.

"There, next to the doctor's case. Do you see it," asked Yakov?

"Yes, I see a strange looking black box, replied the Rabbi. What is it"?

"It is a model 235 electronic muscle stimulator. I must have it for my patients," he said.

In his excitement he slapped the Rabbi three times on his back almost causing him to lose his balance. Yakov peered in the door window, but saw no one inside. Grabbing the handle he rattled the locked door.

63

"Yakov, they are closed today, said the Rabbi. We can come back later."

Yakov pounded on the door as he looked inside. As he pounded harder, a man appeared from the back of the shop.

"Are you mad? Stop pounding on my door. We are closed. Go away," shouted the owner.

As he turned to go back inside Yakov pounded on the door again. The man returned.

"Can't you see or hear? I am closed," he yelled even louder.

"Please sir. I must see that box in the window. It is urgent," begged Yakov.

For a long time the shopkeeper stared at Yakov. Rather than risk a broken glass on his door he reluctantly opened it.

"Show me what you want," he asked.

Yakov, with trembling hands, took the box from the window, and placed it on the counter. He opened the lid and looked in the side compartment. The power cord and electrodes were inside.

"I must have this," Yakov told the rabbi in Russian.

"Ask him how much he wants for it, but say nothing else," replying again in Russian.

Yakov spoke in his slow broken English. "Sir, how much do you want for it," asked Yakov?

The pawnbroker had noticed how badly Yakov wanted the device.

Thinking that he had an easy sale he replied," forty dollars."

Yakov and the Rabbi stepped away from the shopkeeper and discussed his offer.

"Offer him five dollars," whispered the Rabbi.

"I'll give you five dollars for it," said Yakov.

"Are you crazy? Look at the great condition it is in," yelled the broker.

Yakov asked," Do you know what this machine does?"

"No, I don't," he replied.

"In Russia a machine like this was used to electrically torture my father until he died. I must see to it that it is never used like that by anyone here in America," lied Yakov.

The owner wasn't impressed by Yakov suddenly appearing to be overcome by sadness.

"You think I am an idiot. Where did you get that bullshit? OK I'll take thirty dollars," he countered.

The Rabbi and Yakov retreated again and decided on a counter offer.

This time the Rabbi spoke," we'll give you twenty dollars."

"That is an insult. Get out of here before I call the police," he replied.

Yakov and the Rabbi gestured with palms held out to calm the man. Again they huddled to discuss the offer. This time they pretended to argue with each other. With a lot of finger pointing and yelling in Russian they began to wear down the broker's patience.

"Stop it with the Goddamn Russian, he yelled. Give me twenty dollars and get the hell out of here."

Between the Rabbi and Yakov they only had nineteen dollars and thirty six cents. Yakov opened the machine, placed the power cord and the money on the counter. As he held the device to his chest, they walked out the door.

Yelling and swearing at them from the door the shopkeeper threw the cord at them and slammed the door so hard that the glass shattered into a hundred pieces. The Rabbi ran back and picked up the cord. They laughed all the way home.

The stim machine was a big hit with Yakov's patients. For many of them treatment time was cut in half. If his business continued to grow at the rate that it had in the past month, he would be able to buy a new stim machine.

Within a week Yakov, had trained Nadya to use the machine. For Yakov it was a rather painful week. He had offered to play the role of the patient. On three occasions she turned the current knob too high. During one session a powerful jolt sent him sprawling to the floor. Nadya thought it extremely funny. Yakov could only lie on the floor and cuss at her in Russian. Another time she had forgotten to turn the knob to zero before switching on the machine. Yet, even through her own moments of pain she was a fast learner.

On the following Monday, Mr.Lattori was the first patient that Nadya treated with the machine. She knew about his abusive treatment of his wife. Nadya disliked him very much. The two women talked about the possibility of Victoria losing her life. Being married to a mobster boss was her living hell. It was not a partnership in any way. Yes., she kept the books but the mob's bookkeeper oversaw her work. Mrs. Lattori knew that Yakov hated the payoff he had to make on garbage day, but there was nothing she could do. There could be no exceptions.

There was a loud yell from the room Mr. Lattori was in.

"Goddamn you. You try to kill me," he screamed at Nadya.

Yakov burst into the room just as Mr. Lattori was about to strike Nadya. Yakov stepped between them and proceeded to calm him.

"I'm very sorry Mr. Lattori. It was a horrible mistake. Nadya, get Mr. Lattori a glass of wine," Yakov snapped.

As Nadya turned toward the door a smile appeared on her face. When she returned with the wine she apologized to him and left. Yakov finished the treatment.

After Mr. Lattori left he asked Nadya," were you smiling when you left for the wine"?

"What nonsense. I am a doctor. I don't deliberately hurt people," she said.

"It might be better if I attend to Mr. Lattori in the future. It wouldn't be good for us if he died in our care," said Yakov.

In a quiet voice Nadya replied," as you wish, my Lord." They howled with laughter.

October had been a mild month in New York. The pleasant weather carried over into the first week of November. Leonard decided it was time to test the boiler. When the factory was built the owners did not want a coal-burning boiler, with its ash disposal problems. They installed an oil-burning furnace. It was more efficient and easier to maintain. The boiler and oil storage tank were housed in a separate room behind the main building. Leonard drained off the water condensation at the bottom of the fuel tank. The indicator gauge on the tank showed that it was half full. Just to be sure that the oil was ok he drained off a gallon into a glass jug. It showed no contaminants floating around in the oil.

After several attempts to light the pilot light, it finally ignited. Oil came into the fire chamber and burst into a bluish flame. Within a half hour the pressure gauge needle began to move. Steam pressure was building up in the boiler. An hour later he slowly opened the steam valve. He did not open it fully. He wanted to charge the system slowly to see if there were leaks in any of the lines. The used radiators that he had obtained from a demolished building three blocks away showed no signs of leaks. Heat was soon emanating from all of the radiators. The warmth on the first floor of the factory and the office area felt good. There was no heat going to the second story. That valve was kept closed. If there was ever a need for heat up there Leonard was sure that it could easily be done.

Yakov and Nadya could not believe their good fortune. Just a few short months ago they had just a few dollars in their pockets; the Horowitz's were their only friends, and they had a dream. The dream of a chiropractic practice was now a reality. Several of the earliest patients had become their good friends. And the Yakov's bank account was growing.

CHAPTER 12

NADYA'S DISCOVERY

Ever since the birth of their only child Nadya had experienced bouts of pain and genital discomfort. She was able to perform everyday chores but only with the use of some kind of a painkiller. During her heavy labor, delivery of the baby was difficult. Her uterus had torn loose from its normal position. Monthly periods caused excruciating pain. The organ had extended downward into the vagina. During this time heavier doses of drugs were needed to dull the pain. Adding to Yakov's frustration in dealing with Nadya's pain was the fact that intercourse with his beloved wife was totally out of the question. They had not been intimate since the birth of their son Sergi.

One of the reasons that they had come to America was to have Nadya undergo surgery to correct the problem. She could have had it done in Moscow, but Nadya knew that having it done there would put her at great risk. During her medical training she learned how inferior Russian medicine was compared to American medicine. The procedure she needed required great skill and the most modern facility and equipment. Now that the money was available they began to search for the best hospital and surgeon.

From the moment Mrs. Lattori and Nadya first met Nadya felt the presence of her own mother in this Italian woman. Almost instantly there was a bond of trust between them that they both felt. No words could describe it. It just was. And in this moment of crisis for Nadya she turned to her just as she would have turned to her own mother. The pain, the drugs, not being able to fulfill Yakov's desire for her, all came spilling out. Mrs. Lattori held on to her as Nadya sobbed uncontrollably.

When the tears subsided she took Nadya's face in her hands. She looked deeply into her eyes and said, "Tomorrow I will take you to the best doctor in New York. She is my doctor, and if she can't fix you I'll have her shot."

"Can you really do that," asked Nadya in a very serious tone?

"Nadya, I'm joking," she replied. They both laughed heartily. Nadya felt better.

The next day Mrs. Lattori, Nadya, and Yakov went to see Doctor Roberta Finelli After a long examination she assured Nadya that she could perform the surgery. She instructed Nadya and Yakov to be at the hospital just as soon as she was able to make the arrangements. On the fourth day Doctor Finelli called telling them to be at the hospital by 8 o'clock the next day.

Even though Nadya possessed great skills and knowledge as a doctor it did not prevent her from being very nervous. Yakov and Mrs. Lattori did what they could to calm her fears.

The surgery took four hours. After a long wait Doctor Finelli met with Yakov and Mrs. Lattori. She told them Nadya's recovery would take about six weeks. Yakov was handed a list of items that had to be done on a daily basis for Nadya. Mrs. Lattori took it from Yakov's hands.

"I'll take care of this, she said. You go back to work. Nadya will have the best of care."

Four days later Nadya came home. Mrs. Lattori had hired the best caregiver. The woman, Anna, could do it all. She cooked for them; baby sat the boy, cleaned the rooms, did the wash, and cared for Nadya. She never seemed to tire. Yakov commented about the woman's stamina.

Nadya told Yakov, "If the woman doesn't do a good job Mrs. Lattori will have her shot."

Yakov said, "You're joking aren't you."

"No, I'm not," replied Nadya with a straight face. Yakov laughed nervously. He wasn't sure. In Russia it could happen and often did.

The great care that Anna gave Nadya shortened her convalescence by a week. Her doctor was amazed by the progress she had made. Nadya's pain had greatly diminished. She felt that it was time to ask the doctor the question that had troubled her for so long.

"Doctor, when can I have intercourse with my husband? Yakov has waited so patiently," she said.

"Nadya, at this time, if you were to experience just one intense orgasm it would undo all that we have accomplished. As a woman I can understand your frustration. But as two medical professionals we both know that it takes time for those muscles to heal," replied the doctor.

"I pretty much knew what the answer was. But what if I could induce controlled mild orgasms electronically," she asked?

"Nadya, what are you suggesting," asked the doctor?

"Yakov uses a machine called the electronic muscle stimulator in his practice. Muscles are made to contract electrically. The intensity of the contraction is controlled by a knob that raises or lowers the current passing through the muscle. The interval between releasing and contracting of the muscle is set by another knob," explained Nadya.

"That's fine for muscles that lie just beneath the skin. But how do you propose stimulating the uterine muscle," she asked?

"What if we touch one of the electrodes to the clitoris and the other to the base of my skull? With the machine set at its lowest setting we may be able to induce mild orgasmic contractions of the uterus," replied Nadya.

"Nadya, what you are suggesting is very dangerous. How do we know if the contractions will be mild enough not to cause any damage," she asked?

"I am willing to try it. If I feel the slightest twinge of pain we can stop the procedure," Nadya replied.

The doctor did not really want to try this radical approach. But if it did speed up the healing by strengthening the uterine muscles maybe other women could be helped by the technique. They agreed to allow the natural healing to continue over the weekend and undertake the radical approach on Monday morning at the chiropractic facility.

"Do not tell Yakov what we are doing. When I am healed I want to surprise him," said Nadya.

You could see her excitement. She felt like a virgin bride on her honeymoon night.

The doctor arrived early Monday morning. Yakov and the baby were still asleep. Nadya's caregiver was not due to arrive for another hour. She had prepared the examining room that was the furthest from the apartment. A sock was placed next to the stim machine to use as a gag to keep her from yelling out. It would either be a painful or pleasurable sensation.

Nadya had demonstrated to the doctor how the machine worked. She disrobed and lay down on the table. Her knees were slightly raised and spread apart. With her left hand she touched an electrode to her clitoris. The electrode in her right hand she pressed firmly into the base of her skull.

"Turn it on. Now turn the current knob until I tell you to stop," directed Nadya.

The interval knob was already set to about six seconds. She felt the first mild uterine contraction. At the same time a reflex action caused her to raise her head and arch her back slightly off the table.

The doctor turned off the machine before the six-second rest interval had expired.

"How did it feel," she asked?

"It was such a euphoric feeling. There was no pain. I could feel the uterus contract just as if I was having a mild orgasm. The only detraction was the electrode touching the clitoris. It will have to be modified," said Nadya.

They repeated the procedure a dozen times. They increased the rest interval to twenty seconds. At the end of the session Nadya was exhausted. The success of the experiment lifted Nadya's spirits to new heights.

Without telling Leonard anything more than what he needed to know he was able to attach a removable round brass ball to the electrode. With this attachment and some lubricant she was able to stimulate the clitoris even more.

By the end of the first week Nadya was able to do the procedure alone. The doctor cautioned her to proceed slowly. Over the next four weeks she gradually increased the current. She was now having two or three simulated orgasms of such intensity that she could no longer do it every day. It was too exhausting. From the beginning Nadya kept a clinical diary of the experiment. Meticulously she recorded every detail. It would prove to be an invaluable book.

Three entries were especially important. First, she was now totally pain free. The second item she could not medically explain. Her need for pain killing drugs had vanished. There would be almost two decades of brain research before the answer to this question became clear. Brain scientists would discover that during sex the endorphins serotonin and dopamine were released into the brain. They discovered that these chemicals were responsible for the euphoric feeling that an orgasm produced. But in Nadya's case the intense orgasmic like contractions resulted in the release of huge amounts of these two compounds. As the dopamine and serotonin flushed the brain the drug dependency diminished and soon disappeared. Amazingly this happened in a matter of about two weeks.

The third effect had no explanation at all. Nadya felt that no knowledge existed in her head. The void had to be filled. She began reading everything she could find. What was even more amazing her retention of anything she read was extremely high? The phenomenon continued even though she was now using the stim machine only once or twice a week. It was as if her brain had completely rewired itself and was now operating much more efficiently.

This opened a new door for her. Nadya had always wanted to apply for her U.S. medical license. But she was afraid that she could never pass the medical test. Her spoken English was much better than Yakov's, but reading and writing the language was a more difficult hurdle.

CHAPTER 13

DISCOVERED

Nadya's recovery was complete. She was taking a more active part with the patients. Her skill with the stem machine helped Yakov treat more people. The compassion that she gave to all patients endeared her to them. She was like breaths of fresh air to so many that were beaten down by the harsh realities of life. Nadya actually listened to their troubles and offered hope and consolation. She made sure that those who were in need of medical help got the treatment they needed, often paying for it herself. For some of the patients that required surgery she would occasionally ask Mrs. Lattori to intervene financially.

Chiropractic treatment was becoming just one facet of a more holistic medical practice. And the word was rapidly spreading.

Nadya's use of the electronic muscle stimulator on herself was now just an occasional occurrence. One morning when she was using it Yakov had decided to arise early. He noticed Nadya was already up. But this was not unusual as she often got up to check on their son. As he prepared to shower he couldn't help notice that the ceiling light in the bathroom would dim and brighten in a rhythmic pattern. It was the same pattern that he had seen many times before as he used the stim machine on his patients. As the stim machine turned on it put a heavier load on the electrical system causing the bulb to dim. When it paused the bulb brightened again. As he walked down the hallway toward the front of the building, all the examination rooms were open except the one nearest the office. Light was coming into the hall from under the bottom of the door. As he stood next to the door, he could hear soft moaning sounds coming from the room. Slowly he opened the door. He could not believe what he saw. Nadya's eyes were closed and her body was slowly rising up and down, up and down. She was moaning softly each time the stim machine turned on. Yakov felt betrayed. He knew what she doing and it was as if his manhood had been stripped from him. She had not heard him come in.

In a trembling voice he said," Have I failed you as a husband that you needed a machine to replace me?"

"Yakov", she shouted, as she dropped the electrodes to the floor. She sat up and covered her face with her hands.

"I am so ashamed," she said as she wept uncontrollably.

Yakov stood there for several minutes unsure of what to say or do. Finally he sat next to her, wrapped his arms around her, and let her sob. Slowly, between the tears, she began to tell him everything. When she got to the part about the strange use of the stim machine and how it had cured her addiction he was speechless.

"I have no idea how the machine eliminated my need for drugs. My brain feels different. I am more alive than I have ever been. And all of my senses are sharper," said Nadya. She continued," One thing that I am certain of is the contractions of the uterus by the stim machine shortened my recovery by at least two weeks.

"My darling, I had planned to tell you everything on Sunday. That was the day we were going to make love again," she said.

As he looked into her eyes he said," I love you more than I have ever loved anyone."

He slowly lowered her on to the table. At that moment Nadya felt that she was a complete woman again. As she moved her hands over the lean muscles of Yakov's back the intensity of the moment filled her body and mind. She reached down, took his penis in her hand and before she could guide it in her his semen spilled from him.

Yakov cursed in Russian. "I'm so sorry, he said as he sat up. I couldn't hold back."

Nadya sat up next to him. She smiled at him and said," It will be better next time."

She knew he was embarrassed, and she said no more about it.

They cleaned up the table and headed back to their bed room. It was still early. As they walked down the long hallway Nadya was a few steps ahead of him. As she walked he watched the undulating movement of her naked buttock. He was becoming aroused again. By the time they reached the door of their bedroom his penis had new life. He wrapped his arms around her from behind. Nadya giggled as she felt his penis press against her. He turned her around, picked her up, and deposited her on the bed.

Nadya kept the pace of their lovemaking slow to avoid another early release. This time Yakov was able to penetrate her without incident. As he slowly moved in and out Nadya was moaning softly. She moved her body upward as he thrust down driving his penis deeper into her. Nadya accelerated the pace and let out a joyous sound. Her body quivered and convulsed as the intense orgasms consumed her. Yakov could no longer hold back. He pushed deeply into her and released his semen. Three years of frustration melted away. They had become one spirit in that glorious moment of the purest joy that can be shared by a man and woman.

THE BREATH OF FREEDOM

A great burden had been lifted from Nadya's mind. She felt that she was now ready to take a big step forward. Nadya would move on to tackle the next enormous challenge of acquiring her medical license.

CHAPTER 14

NADYA'S DREAM

Ever since their arrival in America Nadya had hoped that someday she would be able to practice medicine in America. She had often spoken with Dr. Finelli about it. Dr. Finelli was very impressed with Nadya's medical knowledge, and she encouraged her to do so. Nervously Nadya picked up the phone and called Dr. Finelli. She told her that she was going to go ahead with her plans.

"Nadya, I will speak with the chief of staff at the hospital and find out what you will need to do, said the doctor. I will call you tomorrow and let you know where we need to start."

"Doctor, I can't thank you enough for your help," said Nadya.

"I'm not doing this just for you, Nadya. In all of New York City, counting me, there are only five female doctors in all of New York City," said Dr. Finelli.

"Why is that," asked Nadya.

"Part of the problem is the attitude among male doctors that females should stay in the home and have babies. That's the way God ordained things and we shouldn't mess with God's will," replied the doctor.

"I would imagine that the male ego also has a lot to do with it," said Nadya.

THE BREATH OF FREEDOM

"Of course it does, said the doctor. You can't imagine how difficult it is for me to deal with that. I face it every day."

Nadya sat quietly for a moment before she responded. "I'm going to do it."

"You're going to face abuse like you have never experienced before. They will pat your butt, rub up against your body, tell you dirty jokes, and try to get you in bed, and yell and scream at you. Being an intern is very hard work. Yakov will feel like you have left him. The hours are very long and you will be deprived of sleep. A woman has to be ready to face all that and more if she is to succeed," she ended her look into Nadya's future.

With a firm determination in her voice Nadya said," I can do this." She slowly hung up the phone.

At the end of office hours and after the last patient had left, Nadya discussed what Dr. Finelli had said with Yakov. Yakov sat in stunned silence.

"Can it really be that way, he asked? How can they get away with such horrible behavior?"

"In Russia medical school was not like that. I was treated with respect, an equal," she said.

"No no, replied Yakov. They lived in fear of the system just as you and I and our families did. Those men knew that you had connections in the government. If anyone of them stepped out of place and you complained to your father he would be gone," said Yakov.

In an angry voice Nadya replied, "I would never had done that."

"Would you have accepted the kind of behavior Doctor Finelli is facing?" asked Yakov.

Nadya, with a pained look on her face, thought long and hard before she answered.

"Yakov, I want to do this. With you and Doctor Finelli by my side I will succeed," she replied.

79

"So many of our patients have connections in high places. Mrs.Lattori would never let anyone harm you," he said.

"I could never ask her for that kind of help. Doctor Finelli has never told anyone about the struggles she faces and neither will I," replied Nadya.

"You expect me to just stand by and do nothing to protect you while those bastards heap abuses on you," he asked?

"Yes", she replied, "that's exactly what I want you to do."

Yakov realized her deep determination to become a doctor in America.

"What we have accomplished together has gone far beyond what I had dreamed we could do in this wonderful country," said Yakov. He continued, "If this is your wish, then some how, some way, we will do it together."

He kissed her on both cheeks and said, "Let's find something to eat. I can't live on love alone."

Nadya grabbed him by the head and gave him a long hard kiss, then whispered in his ear, "I can." At that moment Yakov felt as though the love that he had for this woman would burst his heart and he would die. That night they would subdue their passions.

But the new path that they would take would prevent them from sipping the heady wine of love as much as they had in the past. Time would become their enemy.

At around ten the next morning Doctor Finelli called. "Nadya, can you meet me at the hospital this afternoon at one," she asked?

Nadya replied, "I can be there."

"Good, said Doctor Finelli, I have arranged for you to meet Doctor Anderson. He is head of surgery and in charge of the interns."

Nadya's feminine side kicked in and she asked Doctor Finelli, "What should I wear?"

THE BREATH OF FREEDOM

"Wear something that shows your great figure. He'll look you over and that first impression is critical, she said. Oh, by the way, do you have a small black hat with a light veil?"

"No I don't, she replied. I seldom wear a hat. Why would I need one," she asked?

"When you walk into his office the veil will create an air of mystery about you. He will want to see the face beneath it. His eyes will be on you. After you are seated slowly lift the veil," she explained.

"Why must I play this game? It sounds so silly," replied Nadya.

"Because that is exactly what it is to men, a game. They make the rules of engagement. What women do is embellish the rules to make them work to our advantage," explained Doctor Finelli.

It became clearer to Nadya as she remembered the little things she did whenever she was going to see Yakov. The extra primping and preening must have worked on Yakov. He couldn't take his eyes off her as she prepared for the meeting. It made Nadya so nervous that she had to tell him to stop starring at her.

Dr. Finelli was waiting at the main entrance to the hospital. She had a small box in her hand.

"Hurry, she said. We don't have much time. First we have to stop in the ladies restroom. It's on the twelfth floor just down the hall from Doctor Anderson's office."

"That's a good idea. I'm so nervous I have to go pee," she said.

"Ok, said Doctor Finelli, but we have to put on the hat too."

They looked at each other and laughed like a couple of schoolgirls on their first double date.

They walked into the Doctors office. The girl at the desk was busy talking to another gentleman. When they had finished the secretary spoke.

81

"Doctor Finelli, I'll tell Doctor Anderson that you're here.

"Nadya, I have to get back to work. When you're done stop at the nurse's station on the third floor and ask for me. I want to know how things went," said Doctor Finelli.

The secretary opened the office door and she walked in. She approached Doctor Anderson to shake his hand and introduce herself, when suddenly her right ankle twisted. The high heel of her shoe had skidded on the hardwood floor. He instinctively grabbed her by the arm and kept her from falling. The little black hat fell to the floor. He led her to a chair, and she sat down.

"Are you alright Doctor Yakov? Is your ankle twisted," he asked?

"I'm fine doctor. Thank you. High heels are not my favorite kind of shoes," said Nadya.

"I have really been anxious to meet you. Dr. Finelli has told me a lot of good things about you," he said.

"She has been a great help to me and my husband since she operated on me," said Nadya.

"She told me about the operation. Why didn't you have it done in Russia, he asked? You waited for such a long time to do it."

"Doctor Anderson, you have to understand that medical conditions in Russia are very poor. Sanitation is a joke, and operating rooms are nowhere up to American standards. I simply was afraid to undergo an operation under those conditions," she said.

Doctor Anderson replied," I can certainly understand your hesitation."

This man's behavior was nothing like Doctor Finelli had led her to believe. His eyes had a kind look in them. He looked at her face, not at her breasts, when he spoke to her. She felt very much at ease with him. What she spoke of next was a shock to Doctor Anderson.

THE BREATH OF FREEDOM

"There was another reason why I waited. I have never told anyone about it, not even my husband. My father was a high-ranking naval officer. He was popular and respected by everyone that knew him. His connections got me into medical school. One night he didn't come home. He had been accused of plotting to kill Stalin. There was absolutely no evidence of this, only the rumor. He simply disappeared. When a man falls from favor so does his family. Only through the pleading of my professor was I allowed to stay in school. My fear was that if I was to undergo the procedure I would never awake from the anesthetic. You cannot understand Stalin's brutality and what it is like to live every day in fear. I miss my father everyday," she concluded.

Tears welled up in her eyes. Doctor Anderson walked over to her and sat beside her. He took out his handkerchief and handed it to her. His own eyes were moist. He took her hand in his as she wiped her eyes.

After a few moments Nadya had regained her composure.

"I am so sorry, my dear Nadya," he said.

"As a doctor you know what clinical death is, she said. But there is another death that can be just as fatal, the death of the spirit. When you lose all hope something inside of you dies. America has revived our dead spirits and given us hope again. Each breath that Yakov and I take is filled with the scent of freedom. Most Americans do not know how evil Communism is and what Stalin has done to Russia. We hope that someday soon he will be destroyed and freedom is given back to the people."

"I too hope that day comes soon. But today we must see if we can get you into our intern program. My secretary has prepared all of the paper work that you will have to fill out. The new class starts in two weeks. Get them back to me as soon as possible," said Doctor Anderson.

He escorted her to the door. She thanked him over and over, as she vigorously shook his hand. The elevator ride to the third

83

floor seemed to take forever. Finally the door opened and she could see Doctor Finelli standing at the nurse's station reading a patients chart.

"It must have gone well, she said. You are grinning from ear to ear."

"He was wonderful, Nadya blurted out. The new class starts in two weeks. I have to fill out all these papers."

"I can help you with those. Let me see them," asked Dr. Finelli?

As she was glancing at the papers she stopped and removed one sheet from the stack.

"Nadya, do you know what this paper is," she asked?

"No. I didn't look at any of them," she replied.

"This paper asks if you are a citizen. Did you and Yakov ever file to become American citizens," she asked?

"Yakov and I had often discussed it but we were always so busy with the practice that we just pushed it aside. Can we do it now," she asked?

Doctor Finelli slowly shook her head and said "It takes weeks to prepare for the test. And then you have to wait to be sworn in as new citizens by a federal judge."

"Papa Yakov had told us to become American citizens as soon as we could. But we couldn't seem to find the time," replied Nadya.

Nadya's euphoria came crashing down. "What can we do? The new intern class starts in two weeks."

"The only thing you can do is study for the test and wait for the next class to start," said Doctor Finelli.

"I must hurry home to tell Yakov," said Nadya.

Yakov was surprised at the unexpected turn of events. He had no answers to Nadya's repeated question, "What can we do"?

"In America there is always an answer for any problem," said Yakov.

He wished he could believe what he just said.

THE BREATH OF FREEDOM

"Let's finish up the last patients. Tomorrow we can start looking at the situation with clear heads.

Nadya did not sleep well that night. The next morning she was up early. She busied herself with the chores of preparing the rooms for the day's patients. She finished and sat down at the desk in the office. There was a knock at the door. The office was not open yet. She opened the door to see who it was.

"Gertrude. What a pleasant surprise to see you. Come in," said Nadya.

Since their first momentous encounter over obtaining his license Gertrude had become a loyal friend as well as a patient.

"Nadya. I'm sorry to bother you so early but I am in a lot of pain. As I got out of the tub this morning I slipped and fell, hitting my back on the toilet. While getting up something snapped in my lower back. Can Yakov take a look and see what's wrong," she asked?

"First, let me see if anything is broken," said Nadya.

Nadya poked and prodded and pressed various areas. When she touched the area that Gertrude pointed out she let out a yelp.

"There doesn't seem to be anything broken", said Nadya. "Go into room one and I'll call Yakov."

Nadya returned to the office and turned on the new intercom that Leonard had recently installed. Yakov was still asleep. He awoke grumbling. Nadya explained the situation.

"Tell her I'll be there as quickly as I can," he said.

Nadya returned to the room where Gertrude was. While they waited for Yakov she noticed that Nadya wasn't her usual self.

"Nadya, she said, you are not a happy person. What's wrong," she asked? I can see it in your face, tell me now."

"I'm fine Gertrude. Everything is fine," she meekly replied.

85

Nadya continued, "Gertrude, you don't need to be worrying about my problems. Let's get you well."

"Tell me or I'll find another chiropractor guy," Gertrude's voice was sharper now.

"You'd never go. You love Yakov too much," replied Nadya.

"Alright, I confess that's true, now tell me what it is that's bothering you," she asked in a quiet, comforting voice.

Nadya told her the whole story as tears filled her eyes. When she had finished Gertrude was deep in thought. After a moment had passed, Gertrude spoke.

You be at my office tomorrow at one o'clock. We'll see what can be done. Now put a smile back on your face and tell pretty boy to get his ass in here," she growled through her pain.

Just then Yakov came into the room.

"What were you girls talking about? As I got to the door I heard Gertrude say something about pretty boy's ass. Does she have a new boyfriend," he asked?

The girls howled with laughter even though Gertrude's pain was killing her.

The next day Nadya arrived at Gertrude's office promptly at one. There were five people seated and one at the counter. Gertrude noticed Nadya as she came in. She seated herself in an empty chair around the corner from the counter. As Gertrude concluded her business with the gentleman at the counter, she stood up and promptly announced," I'm sorry folks, but I have to leave. I have been informed that there has been a death in the family. Please come back tomorrow."

Slowly the remaining five trudged toward the door. The last guy in line turned around and said," The phone never rang. How were you informed about the death?

"See that pigeon on my window sill. It was carrying a note in its beak. Now get the hell out so that I can grieve in peace," she said sarcastically.

He slammed the door as he left.

"Gertrude, that was a terrible lie," Nadya said with a laugh.

"Gertrude, how are you feeling today?" Asked Nadya?

"I'm much improved. Thanks for asking. Pretty boy really knows his stuff," she commented. Gertrude removed a bottle of Jack Daniels whiskey and two glasses from the bottom drawer of her desk. She placed them in a paper bag.

"What is that for," asked Nadya?

"Jack and I and another unnamed guy are going to have a party, said Gertrude. I'll be back in about an hour. You wait here and lock the door when I leave."

It was almost two hours before she returned. Gertrude pounded on the door.

"Open up. It's me," she whispered.

Nadya opened the door and caught Gertrude as she stumbled in. She clutched the paper bag in her right hand. She handed it to Nadya.

"Open it, open it," she said.

In the bag was an envelope. Nadya opened the envelope. As she read the paper she was stunned. It was a formal document, stating, that on this date, Nadya Yakov, was a naturalized citizen of the United States of America. It was signed by Federal Judge Leland Morgan.

"Gertrude, how did you do this," asked Nadya in an astonished voice?

"Let's just say that I have a great power over men, slurred Margaret. He was an animal but I tamed him. Besides, we used to date."

Nadya held on to her as Gertrude reached over and opened a door that led to a side room. Inside was a small bed. She pointed to it and Nadya laid her down on it.

"Gertrude, what a remarkable woman you are," said Nadya.

Gertrude didn't hear her. She had passed out.

CHAPTER 15

A NEW HEADING

With the completion of the entrance papers Nadya started her internship on September10, 1940. From the beginning things unfolded pretty much as Doctor Finelli had explained. The sexual harassment was almost a daily thing.

But as the days wore on things began to change. The old boys club began to recognize that Nadya was much more than just a pretty face. She consistently scored higher than any of the interns on the periodic exams. During patient rounds she answered questions faster and in more detail, often leaving the doctor in charge with his mouth open.

During cram sessions all the other interns wanted to be in her study group. They worked up a schedule so that no one group monopolized all of her time. The doctors at the hospital could see a definite improvement in the skills of the other interns. She was making them better.

There was no doubt that the training and education Nadya had received in Russia was good. It was the communist system that failed to support the medical community. Many of the top leaders of the party often went to London to get treated for illnesses.

By September of 1941, Nadya had completed all of the requirements. Normally the intern program was set up to last four years. But Doctor Anderson felt that she was ready to take her final exam. It was a grueling six-hour ordeal. She had actually finished in five hours, but she went back and rechecked every answer.

Almost a month went by with out any word on how she had done on the exam. Everyone she knew asked her every day if she had heard yet. It was absolutely maddening.

Suddenly it was over. As she entered the hospital to work her shift, people she knew would smile at her and greet her with a warm hello. Some people just shook her hand vigorously without saying a word. When she reached the ward and walked through the door there was a loud cheer. Patients must have fallen out of their beds from all the commotion. Dr. Anderson came over to her, shook her hand, hugged her, and said, "Congratulations Doctor Yakov."

He handed her a gift. "Open it," he said.

Her hands shook as she tore open the paper. She held in her hand her New York State medical license in a beautiful frame. She held it up for everyone to see as the tears ran down her face. Suddenly Yakov was standing next to her holding a beautiful bouquet of flowers. In the crowd she saw Leonard, Gertrude, and the Horowitz's, Doctor Finelli, Mrs. Lattori, and several of New York City's men in blue. Interns from her class were everywhere. Dr. Anderson had heard from the regency board that Nadya had passed the test the day before. He told Dr. Finelli the good news. She managed to call everyone that knew Nadya. The next day they were all there at the hospital.

Doctor Anderson raised his arms and asked the crowd for quiet. When the din had stopped he asked Doctor Nadya Yakov to speak. She was helped on to a chair so that all could see and hear her.

Nadya began to speak." Dear friends, in the three short years that Yakov and I have been here in America our lives have changed so dramatically. It was literally like being reborn. We came from a system of government that instilled nothing but fear in the hearts of its people. Most of you here today have never had the thought that today may be your last day on earth. In Russia our souls had died.

When we arrived at the Amsterdam station and stood among the throngs of people it was as if we were living a dream. We were stunned and shocked; we couldn't move nor speak. Our senses became overwhelmed. We took a deep breath. It was the smell of sausages, coming from a vendor's cart that awakened us. He had seen that we were frightened. He reached out and shook our hand. His smile assured us that that we had nothing to fear. It was at that moment that we learned what freedom was. Freedom is simply one human being reaching out to help another without the fear of death hanging over both of you.

Many of you here today reached out to us in our times of struggle. You helped us learn the many little things that are involved in being free. Yakov and I thank you for that. You have helped us find where freedom lives. It lives in each individual that reaches out to help someone. It lives in you. Thank you so much."

Yakov helped Nadya down from the chair. There wasn't a dry eye in the place as everyone yelled and cheered. Many of the lights on the patient's callboard were lit. It was time to go back to work.

Nadya had joined the doctor's old boys club as their equal.

During the rest of 1940 Nadya settled into a routine of seeing patients and helping with the chiropractic business. But it soon became apparent that her own rapidly growing practice had to be her main focus. It was time to speak to Yakov about the situation.

THE BREATH OF FREEDOM

"Yakov, we must hire a new assistant. Working at the hospital and helping here is tiring me to the point of exhaustion. I must put my patients first," she carefully explained.

A smile crossed Yakov's face.

"I agree. I spoke with Rabbi Horowitz after last Sunday's supper. He has a new family from Latvia at the synagogue. He said they remind him of us when we first arrived," said Yakov.

"Why didn't you tell me," Nadya asked.

"I wanted to meet her and see if she would be right for the job before I told you about her," he replied.

She was an experienced secretary from the city of Riga.

"Did she pass inspection," asked Nadya?

"Yes she did. She's young and beautiful. I have fallen in love with her and we are leaving for Russia next week. Would you like to meet her? She will be her this afternoon," kidded Yakov.

"I can't. I have patients to see at the hospital today," replied Nadya.

"If she works out, you can meet her later," he said.

Nadya was relieved that Yakov would have the help that he needed. She was also glad that she would have more time for her own practice.

Two weeks had passed. Sasha, the new girl, was a quick study. She was learning very quickly and would have jumped in front of a bus if Yakov asked her to. To start Yakov was paying her five dollars a week. Her gratitude for this chance to work was boundless. Yakov was familiar with those feelings.

One day Sasha came to work and brought her husband, Dimitri Carpov, and Rabbi Horowitz with her. The Rabbi had no idea why they had asked him to come.

Sasha shyly approached Yakov, took his hand and placed two five-dollar bills in it.

91

Dimitri said," Mister Yakov, it is a man's place to care for his family. We feel that we cannot accept your money. She will gladly work for nothing until I am able to support her."

No amount of persuasion from Yakov or the Rabbi could change his mind.

Yakov admired the pride of this man.

He thought for a moment and said," Everybody wait here."

When he returned Leonard was with him. He had been working on the second floor.

"Your husband now has a job. He will start today working for Leonard. Dimitri said that he has a little skill in the building trades. What ever else he needs to know Leonard will teach him. Here is your ten dollars back for the two weeks you have worked. Thank you for coming Rabbi. Now everybody get to work," said Yakov as he walked out the door.

Sasha, Dimitri and the Rabbi were very pleased with the outcome. The Rabbi wasn't sure why his presence was even needed. But he was happy about the outcome. They heard Yakov shout once more" get to work."

CHAPTER 16

THE PERMANENT PATIENT

Yakov had not slept well that night and had risen early. Nadya was sleeping soundly when he left the room. He walked down the hall to the office. Yakov opened the front door and stepped outside. The wind had a cold cutting edge to it. Canadian air had settled over New York, and with it came unusually lower temperatures for October. In Russia, at this time of year, it was probably snowing. Stretching his arms high into the air he breathed deeply.

As he turned to go back inside a voice startled him. Yakov looked around and saw no one. He left the front stoop and, as he walked toward the corner of the building, he heard it again. Cautiously he slowly peeked around the edge of the brick wall. Sitting on the ground was a woman. Her back was against the wall and she was making incoherent sounds. It wasn't unusual to occasionally find a drunk passed out, but it was odd to find a woman here.

Yakov knelt down on one knee next to her. She smelled terrible. Her eyes were closed. She had been beaten about the face and head.

"Can I help you," he asked. In his excitement he spoke to her in Russian.

There was no response. He asked again, "Can I do anything for you?"

She continued to utter words that made no sense. Her breathing was very shallow. He didn't know what to do.

Yakov said, still speaking Russian, "Don't move. I'll be right back."

He ran back into the office, turned on the intercom and yelled, "Nadya, come to the office, and hurry"

He returned to the woman's side. Yakov held her hand. It was cold as ice. Nadya arrived and knelt next to her. She could see that the woman was in trouble Nadya had many questions. But they would have to wait to be asked. She didn't have a scrap of paper on her. And there was no purse.

"We must get her out of the cold. Let's carry her inside," said Nadya.

They carried her into the first examination room and gently laid her on the table.

"I'll clean her up. Go get towels and some hot water," she ordered.

The woman had soiled herself and was wet with urine. Nadya undressed her. Yakov returned with the items. Nadya washed the feces and urine from her body. She appeared to be in her middle twenties.

"What should we do with her," asked Yakov?

"I don't know, replied Nadya. For now let's just try to warm her up and see if we can get her to take some hot soup."

"It's almost time to open up. We can move her to the second floor. Leonard has finished the first room and he has the heat on up there. He has already put in a bed," said Yakov.

"I'll take the morning off, said Nadya. She stepped out to the office and called Dr. Finelli to make the arrangements. We will have to find someone to stay with her for a while," she replied.

They put her on a gurney and wheeled her to the elevator.
On the second floor she was rolled into the completed room.
Over the rest of the second floor Leonard had material scattered
everywhere. He was in the process of building more rooms. As
they made the woman comfortable Leonard arrived.

"Doctor Yakov", said Leonard, I need to talk to you. I don't
know how to make the rooms soundproof"

Yakov responded," never mind that for now. Nadya and I
need your help. The woman that we have in this room is very ill.
Doctor Nadya will be with her this morning. You and Dimitri
find something to do at the other end of the building. Try to be
as quiet as you can."

Nadya had returned from the kitchen with some soup.

"Yakov, hold her up and I'll feed her," directed Nadya.
Yakov sat her up while Nadya held her head, opened her
mouth, and spooned in a small amount. She didn't gag and
Nadya felt her swallow. She managed to get her to take a little
bit more. As she was about to try one more spoon full she
stopped.

Nadya whispered, "Yakov, her eyes are open."

"Hello", she said softly. "My name is Doctor Yakov. This is
my husband. Can you hear me?"

The woman slowly nodded yes. Nadya raised the spoon
and offered her more of the soup. She managed to eat a little
more, and then stopped.

"Where am I," she asked, just above a whisper?

"You are in our medical office. Early this morning we found
you outside our office lying unconscious on the ground. What
is your name?" asked Nadya.

She thought for a long while. She began crying softly as her
body trembled.

She could not answer.

Nadya held her hand and said, "You had been beaten about the head. That may have caused you to have a temporary loss of memory. Gradually you will remember things."

"I have to leave now. Thanks for helping me," said the woman.

She got out of the bed and stood up before Nadya could stop her. The mystery patient immediately passed out and sank to the floor. Nadya called to Yakov, who had gone to speak to Leonard. He ran back to the room and helped Nadya put her back in bed.

"She will not be able to stand until the swelling on her head goes down. We must keep her in bed until then," said Nadya.

'Maybe Leonard can make some soft restraints to hold her on the bed," suggested Yakov.

"I hate to do that. We use them on patients at the hospital to keep them from hurting themselves. But only as a last resort," said Nadya.

Yakov called Leonard who was working at the far end of the building. With a series of gestures and broken English the carpenter conveyed to Dimitri what he was to do until he got back.

Yakov tried to explain to Leonard in his broken English what restraints were. Nadya's English was much better than Yakov's. But it was too difficult a concept for Leonard to understand. They decided to call Rabbi Horowitz to see if he could come over. Within an hour he arrived.

"Rabbi, we are trying to get Leonard to understand that we need a bed that will keep a patient safe by restraining her," said Nadya.

Even the Rabbi had a hard time trying to put this idea into English.

"Leonard, the Yakov's need a special bed that has straps on it that attach to a patience's hands and feet so that the patient cannot get out of bed," explained the Rabbi.

"Is the person crazy?" asked Leonard.

Rabbi Horowitz translated Leonard's question. Nadya shook her head no.

"We know she has used drugs. There appear to be needle marks on her arms. There is no way to tell when she had her last fix. When the drugs wear off she may become violent. She also has a head injury. If she gets up it could cause damage to her brain. We need to sedate her. We cannot let her get out of bed until she is stable. And someone has to stay with her," explained Nadya.

Leonard, mentally, had begun working on the problem of the restraints. As he turned to leave Nadya cautioned him.

"Leonard, no one is to know she is here. We are going to try and help her," Nadya said. He promised not to tell a soul and left.

As an extra precaution Nadya prepared a syringe that contained a drug that would put her into a light sleep. She injected the sedative. It would sedate her and keep her calm. But it would not put her under completely. This way she hoped to get the woman's name and where she lived.

"Sasha should be here by now, said Yakov. I'll get started with the day's patients. As soon as I get a chance I'll check on you and the lady."

"See how Leonard is doing with the restraints," asked Nadya?

"I'll see if I can find him," Yakov replied.

Sasha was amazing. She had patients signed in and some already assigned to various examination rooms waiting for Doctor Yakov. She was developing the ability to anticipate what the doctor would need for each patient's visit. This contributed to an efficient, smooth running office.

She was about to leave the office to go check on a patient in one of the exam rooms. Yakov stopped her.

"Where is Leonard," he asked?

She pointed to the front door and said," he left about ten minutes ago."

"Did he say where he was going?" asked Yakov.

"No. But he did say he'd be back in about an hour," said Sasha.

"Find me as soon as he returns," replied Yakov.

Leonard had gone to General Hospital. He had never seen restraints and was looking for information on what they looked like. He entered the lobby. The girl at the information desk asked if she could help him find what he was looking for.

"Yes, he said. I' m here to do research on the use of bed restraints."

"Are you writing a paper for your school," she asked.

"No, he said. I'm with the City Health Department looking into the complaint that many patients are put in restraints and left unattended for long periods of time. I want to see how they are used here."

Leonard was as slick as oil. The receptionist proceeded to help him.

"There are several gurneys parked down at the end of that hallway that have restraints on them. She pointed at the corridor to her right. I'll get someone to help you."

"That won't be necessary, he replied. I just want to get a good look at them. Thank you for your help."

He scurried down the hall and as he passed a laundry cart he grabbed a pillow case from it. He approached the gurneys. One of the carts had restraints that were made from sheepskin leather. He looked under the cart to see how they were attached. Leonard reached into his pocket and took out a small knife. He glanced around to see if anyone was watching. No one was there. With quick slashes of the knife he cut the four leather straps as close to where they were attached to the cart as he could.

Leonard closed the knife and slipped it back into his pocket. He scooped the restraints into the pillowcase and slowly walked back to the entrance and left the building.

He entered Yakov's building by the back door. At the top of the stairs he picked up his tool box and proceeded to the exam room.

By ten he had the restraints firmly attached to the woman's bed. Leonard was surprised that the woman never moved a muscle during the installation of the restraints. He installed them pretty much as they were attached on the hospital gurney. Leonard didn't feel any guilt over what he had done. To him it was just another way to survive the depression.

Around 10:30 Nadya called Victoria Lattori and asked her if she could send over Anna, the woman that had stayed with Nadya during her surgery recovery. By 11:00 she was there.

"Anna, this woman is very ill. She has a severe head wound. Right now she is drugged. We need to keep her very still. If she comes to and tries to get up she could die. We have these restraints on her to keep her in bed," said Nadya.

"What happened to her," asked Anna.

"We don't know, replied Nadya. Yakov found her lying on the ground early this morning. If she regains consciousness she will be very frightened. I have to go to the hospital for my rounds. Try to tell her that she must be very still and that she is very ill. We will take off the restraints if she lies still."

By the time Yakov's last patient left, the woman of mystery had not moved. Her breathing was shallow but not stressed.

"Thank you for coming Anna, said Yakov. I will stay with her. Nadya will be here soon and she can examine her."

"I will fix you some supper before I go. If the lady awakes she will need some of my special soup too," said Anna.

Anna's soup warmed Yakov and lifted his spirits. By the time she finished doing the dishes it was after 9 o'clock. She said "good night" and left.

Nadya arrived a few minutes after Anna had left. She ate a little of the soup that was left and went up to the second floor of the factory. She kissed Yakov on the cheek and asked," How has she been?"

Yakov replied," There doesn't seem to be any change. I don't know how much longer she can go without food or water."

"I know, said Nadya. I have been thinking of a solution. I want to use the stim machine on her."

Yakov looked at her with disbelief.

"Nadya, we can't do that. Using the machine on you was different than using it on a patient that can't accept or reject the idea. We could both lose our licenses."

"What should we do? Just sit here and watch her die. Yakov, I know this will work on her too. Right now she cannot be moved. It could kill her if we tried."

Yakov put his hands on Nadya's shoulders. He looked into her eyes and said, "Nadya, we could lose all that we have worked so hard for. We must turn her over to the hospital in the morning."

She pleaded," I can't Yakov. I can't. Let me try just one treatment. If she does not respond I'll do as you say,"

Yakov walked over to the bed. He looked at the woman's face for a moment.

Without turning his gaze He asked," When would we do this?"

"We could do it now, tonight," Nadya responded excitedly.

"I'll go get the machine," he replied in a quite voice.

CHAPTER 17

The Turning Point

Nadya had positioned the woman so the electrode could be inserted into the vagina with the least amount of discomfort. The other electrode was attached to the base of the head slightly to the left of center. Nadya had retrieved the journal that she had written during the time of her healing. She set the current level to the lowest setting and the interval knob to ten seconds. These were the settings that she had recorded in her journal.

She held the vaginal electrode in place and turned on the machine. As the first pulse of current entered the woman's body a slight convulsive movement occurred. As the ten second lapse started she relaxed. The next pulse induced a slightly stronger contraction. Nadya adjusted the time interval to fifteen seconds to give her body a longer rest period.

Nadya turned off the machine. The woman's respiration was faster and deeper. Her blood pressure measured higher.

"She's responding well. I'm going to turn up the current a little," said Nadya.

Yakov pointed to the woman's eyes that were still closed. "There seems to be a rapid movement of her eyes under the lids," said Yakov.

"That's good. It shows that the brain is being stimulated," replied Nadya.

She inserted the electrode and turned on the machine. This time the convulsive reactions were stronger. In the middle of the third charge the woman suddenly opened her eyes and let out a deep moan. Nadya turned off the machine. Two more small shudders went through her body. The woman was calm as she glanced around the room. She gave a tug at the restraints but did not fight them.

Nadya quietly spoke to the woman. "We want you to lie very still. I am a doctor and I am using a new treatment on you. It will help you to heal faster and the need for drugs will disappear. The head wound you received is very serious. You have been in a coma for most of the day."

All the while that Nadya spoke she was gently brushing back the hair on the woman's forehead with her hand.

Nadya asked," can you tell us your name"?

Nadya could feel the muscles on the woman's forehead tighten. Tears ran down her cheeks, and her lips formed the word "no".

"Sh sh sh. It's OK. It's OK. It will come back to you. As the swelling on your head goes down you will remember your name. Do you understand what I am saying?", she asked.

Nadya was about to ask again when she heard the woman reply, "Yes."

"I must ask you one more question. Do we have your permission to continue the treatments"?

Again she replied with a very quiet, "yes."

"Thank you," replied Nadya.

As Yakov and Nadya were about to leave, the woman raised her right arm as far as the restraint would allow and held it there.

"No", said Nadya. We can't take the chance of you falling out of bed. Tomorrow we'll put you in a bed that has side rails, and the restraints can be removed. Let's all get some sleep now. We will see you in the morning.

As Nadya and Yakov prepared for bed, Yakov asked, "Now that she is awake maybe this would be a good time to admit her to the hospital?"

"Yakov, I don't think she can be moved safely right now, replied Nadya. And besides, you saw the way she behaved. I think we should continue with the treatments."

"She is putting a strain on us that we can't respond to. The demands on our time are keeping us from doing our jobs," he heatedly replied.

"You are right, Yakov, but what if we can save her life? What if we can make her whole again? Think of what we could do for other women," she replied.

Yakov nearly exploded. "What do you mean, other women? How can we take on more than what we are already doing? It's simply not possible," he replied frantically.

Nadya waited for Yakov to calm down. She sat beside him on the bed and held his hand. She looked at him for a long time. He finally turned his head and looked at her.

He spoke first. "You always do this to me. I yell. You wait. And in the end you always win."

"Sometimes I let you win," she replied.

He laughed as he said, "The last time I won we were still in Russia."

"We'll figure something out. You'll see," said Nadya.

The next morning there was a chill in the air. November was almost over and Nadya was putting her plan to work.

It was early but she knew Victoria Lattori was awake.

Nadya dialed the phone. "Hello Vicky. This is Nadya."

After the usual pleasantries were exchanged, Nadya got to the reason for the call.

"Vicky, is Anna available for a period of about six weeks?," asked Nadya.

"Hold the line. She's here now. I'll go ask her," replied Mrs. Lattori.

Nadya continued," Ask her if she could start today"?

After a short time Mrs. Lattori was back on the line. "She can be there by nine," she replied.

"That's fine. I'll be here at the office. When I see you I'll explain why I need her," she said.

She left the office and went up to the second floor to check on the patient. Sasha was in the room with her. Standing by the bed Sasha whispered to Nadya that the lady was sleeping soundly. Nadya checked the woman's pulse.

Nadya nodded and left the room. Leonard and Dimitri were quietly talking at the far end of the factory's second floor. She called to Leonard, and he started walking toward her.

"Leonard, she said, we need you to build four more rooms as quickly as you can. The rooms are to be as soundproof as you can make them. We will also need a bathroom with a shower installed on this floor."

"I'll draw up the plans tonight," he responded.

"No", said Nadya, "drop what you are doing and get started on this as soon as you can."

Leonard responded to the urgency in her voice, "I'll get started right away Mrs.Yakov."

Leonard returned to where Dimitri was working and explained to him the change of plans.

By the next day materials had been ordered and work on the heating system had begun. Leonard had contacted Margaret to obtain the necessary building permits. According to Nadya's instructions all the work had to be conducted as quietly as possible for the sake of the patient at the far end of the building. This made his work difficult. (it seems impossible to me)

THE BREATH OF FREEDOM

Anna arrived early and Sasha returned to her duties downstairs. Anna and Nadya entered the patient's room. Nadya closed the door and placed two chairs next to each other, and they sat down. She explained to Anna how this woman had come to be in the only finished room on the second floor.

"What I am about to tell you must not be repeated to anyone." She swore Anna to secrecy.

Nadya explained to Anna how the use of the stim machine had cured her of drug addiction. She proceeded to tell Anna that she was presently using the machine on the unknown patient. Nadya gave Anna the option of staying and helping her with the treatments or returning to Mrs. Lattori.

Anna looked for a long time at the patient. It was hard for her to believe that this woman had been so brutally attacked.

She turned to Nadya and said, "I will do everything that you ask me to do to help this poor soul."

While they talked the woman began to stir. When she opened her eyes Nadya could see that she was confused. She held her hand and spoke softly to her. She again explained where she was. Nadya surmised that the patient had not retained all that she had told her on the previous day. The woman grew calm as Nadya explained how and why she was there. When Nadya had finished explaining the stim machine treatment she again asked the patient if she would allow her to use it. The woman nodded yes.

Nadya attached the machine to the patient as Anna watched. Anna had doubts that a simple machine could cure anyone. But she was also curious as she had never experienced an orgasm with a man. For most women talking about orgasms was too personal and embarrassing a subject. Who ever heard of a woman say that she had actually enjoyed having sex. Anna was totally confused but she trusted Nadya completely.

Nadya turned on the machine. It had been set to a low current and as it began stimulating the clitoris the patient's

105

body reacted and she convulsed into a mild orgasm. Nadya stopped the treatment.

"Did you have any head pain?" asked Nadya. The woman quietly responded, "No."

Nadya had asked about head pains because of the severe injuries that the patient had received to her head.

To Nadya's surprise the patient said," do it again."

Nadya turned up the current slightly but decreased the interval knob. After four more orgasms she turned off the machine and removed the electrodes.

"You must rest now. We will give you another treatment this evening," said Nadya.

There was a knock on the door. Leonard had arrived pushing a new hospital bed, complete with clean sheets and side rails. Nadya and Anna removed the restraints from the patient, transferred her to the bed, and raised the side rails. The woman immediately went into a deep sleep.

Outside the room Nadya called to Leonard and was about to ask him where the bed came from. On second thought she decided it would be best if she didn't.

Instead she said," The work is coming along nicely. The new radiators have added a lot of warmth up here. Thank you, Leonard."

Leonard replied," thank you, mum." He turned and went back to work.

Anna and Nadya soon were into a routine. The patient was receiving three treatments a day and she was responding well. Anna's soup was helping to restore her strength. She was able to stand for short periods without passing out. The head trauma had greatly improved.

One day during the fourth week of treatments, as the woman was resting, she began to cry. Anna was alone with her.

Anna took her hand and asked, "What's wrong?"

The woman squeezed Anna's hand and pulled Anna to her.

Softly she told Anna, "My name is Mary Dawson. I was born in Syracuse. I lived in a house on 35 Jackson Street. My mother's name is Frieda. Daddy's name was Frank. He died when I was twelve."

Anna pulled Mary upright and held her tightly. They both cried until Mary started shouting," I remember everything. Everything has come back."

Mary said it over and over. Anna lowered her back to the bed.

"We must tell Doctor Yakov right away," said Anna.

"No. No. I want to do it," said Mary.

Nadya had just returned from the hospital. As she walked into the office Sasha told her that Anna had asked that she come to the patient's room as soon as she got in.

Nadya cursed the slow speed of the elevator. She rushed to the door, opened it, and walked over to Anna. She was ready to face what ever the situation was.

Anna was trying hard to keep a somber look on her face as she said," the patient wishes to speak to you."

Mary was sitting in a chair. Nadya walked over to her. Mary slowly stood up, extended her hand and said," "hello Doctor Yakov. My name is Mary Dawson. I am twenty two years old, and I want to thank you for saving my life."

Through her tears Nadya replied," Thank you Mary. I have waited a long time to meet you."

That night Nadya told Yakov of the breakthrough. And of course she added the dreaded remark, "I told you so."

CHAPTER 19

FAMILY

Yakov's and Nadya's extended family now included Mary. After seven weeks of treatments she had fully returned from the brink of death. Nadya had slowly reduced the use of the stim machine. It had been a week since her last treatment. Mary tired easily in the afternoon, but she was growing stronger everyday.

The Sunday dinners began in the first year shortly after Yakov started the practice. It included some of the first patients that Yakov and Nadya had met. It was always an open-ended affair usually lasting long into the night. If you had the time you just showed up, but you had to bring something for the party. Often guests would bring ethnic dishes related to their family. They all gathered in the Horowitz's basement.

The Horowitz's family, Margaret, several policemen, the Italian lady, Mrs. Lattori, and others often attended. To Yakov every new patient was a new friend and through the years the party grew.

One of Yakov's patients, who was also a Russian immigrant, had opened a restaurant. He had difficulty obtaining a license, just as Yakov had experienced. Once again Margaret became the heroine. To show his gratitude he asked Yakov to move the party to his place. Rabbi Horowitz's wife was delighted with the idea. The place was roomy; the food was excellent. It was in this

108

setting that Nadya was going to reacclimate Mary Dawson back into the world.

On Saturday Nadya and Mary were going shopping. She was going to take her to a little shop that Mrs. Lattori had found on Fifth Avenue. When Nadya told Mrs. Lattori about the plans to buy Mary some new clothes, Mrs. Lattori insisted that she come along. Mary had no idea where they were going. Promptly at nine o'clock Victoria's car and driver arrived to pick Nadya and Mary up. It was Mary's first meeting with Victoria. Nadya of course, had kept Mrs. Lattori informed on Mary's progress every week.

To Mary it was like a visit to her favorite aunt. As a child she remembered the visits to Aunt Tessa's house in South Syracuse. As Mary approached the car, Victoria jumped out, wrapped her arms around her, and smothered her with kisses and a hug.

When Victoria finally released Mary she said," I have waited so long to meet you. Nadya has told me all about you. The three of us are going to have some fun to celebrate. God's love saved you, and now He has turned you over to me.

"Get in girls. Move it Tony. It's time to party," said Vicky.

Mary felt like she had been covered with a warm fuzzy blanket. She experienced the same attraction that Nadya felt the first time that she met Mrs. Lattori. Many Italian women possessed this charm. The overpowering personality, combined with a joy for life, made her irresistible.

The next day, at the Sunday gathering, Mrs. Lattori made sure everyone was introduced to Mary. She looked stunning in the new dress and the new hairdo that Mrs. Lattori insisted Mary needed. Mary soon felt at ease with everyone, and with great urging from the crowd she was forced to say a few words.

"I am happy to be here and to meet all of you. The love and kindness that I have been given has brought me more happiness than I have ever known. Nadya and Yakov gave me back my life. I am forever grateful to them," she concluded.

As the tears appeared in her eyes Yakov jumped up and said," This is a party not a funeral. Let us raise our glasses and drink to life, happiness for us all, and to freedom."

They celebrated long into the night.

CHAPTER 19

THE NEW ARRIVALS

The war years, 1941 to 1945, were very hard on Gerog and Katrina, Yakov's parents. Hitler's invasion of Russia had been a disaster for the Germans. Gerog, despite his age, was at the front lines in Leningrad. It was a battle of huge destructive proportions. The number of dead was in the thousands. The Germans were defeated, not just by bombs and bullets but also by the weather. Russia had been hit by the worst winter in fifty years. Many German soldiers froze to death holding their weapons in their hands. The Russians were used to cold winters and knew how to survive.

On the morning of June 26, 1946, in New York City, the phone rang in Yakov's office. Yakov picked up the phone. The caller identified himself as Minister Petroff at the Russian Consulate. Minister Petroff's voice sounded strange.

"Comrade Yakov, please come to the consulate as soon as possible. It is urgent that I see you. I have news of your father," said the minister.

Yakov replied," I will leave as soon as I speak to my wife."

Yakov and Nadya arrived at the consulate. As he stood at the bottom of the steps there remained, deep inside him, that lingering fear. As they entered the building he remembered that day so long ago when he stood outside filled with such a fear

111

that it almost choked him. Everything was exactly the same. Minister Petroff had remained at his post all through the war years. There was not a hue of color to be seen anywhere. The consulate's interior was exactly the same as it was in 1938, dull, dreary, and drab.

The secretary hurried to Petroff's door the instant that Yakov arrived and just as quickly she returned.

"The minister will be right out," she said. She appeared to be nervous and fidgety.

Yakov thought it strange that he would come out of his office to speak to him.

The minister walked over to where Yakov was standing. He grabbed him by the shoulders and kissed him on both cheeks. Yakov was stunned. The smile on the minister's face led Yakov to believe he had good news. Yakov could never have guessed what he was about to see.

He led Yakov to the closed door of the inner office. They stopped at the door. Minister Petroff opened the door and allowed Yakov to enter. Four people, with their backs turned, were standing in front of the minister's desk. As the four turned around to face Yakov he immediately recognized his mother and father. He could not speak or move. The tears in his eyes blinded him.

"Have you become so Americanized that you have no feelings for your father and mother?", asked Gerog.

Yakov rushed to them, and they embraced. They held on to each other and their tears running down all their cheeks mingled as they kissed again and again. Yakov turned to the other two women and pulled them into the circle. The kissing started all over again. Gerog started singing an Old Russian folk song about family. Everyone joined in. Yakov noticed Minister Petroff's voice could be heard above all the others. From shear exhaustion they all sat down. Gerog and Yakov sat together in the far corner of the room.Gerog began explaining how they were able to leave Russia.

Before the Germans arrived in Russia Gerog had been able to exchange messages with Yakov and Nadya by courier mail through the New York Russian Consulate. But Gerog's deployment to the front prevented communicating with Yakov.

When the war was finally over, Gerog returned to his work at the Kremlin. Both of his secretaries had survived the war and were anxious to get back to work.

A week after his return Gerog went to Major Sakov's office. It was still in the basement of the building. Several soldiers, their uniforms in tatters, faces dirty, and eyes that looked dead from seeing the horrors of war, were seated at the table. What little talking they did was in quiet hushed tones.

Gerog asked to speak to Major Sakov. Two of the men started weeping softly at the mention of his name.

The soldier seated nearest to Gerog spoke," The Colonel was killed four weeks ago in Leningrad. He died a hero. The Germans had us in machine gun crossfire. He attacked their position with grenades and killed them all. As he walked along the road back to our position he stepped on a land mine. It blew him to pieces. He was like a brother to us."

Gerog was shocked at the news.

"He was a hero to me also. He once saved my life. A more trusted friend you could never find. I am deeply grieved by our loss," said Gerog.

What Gerog had never told anyone about his friendship with Uri Sakov was that he and Uri had smuggled out of Russia 127 people that were on the Communist party list to be executed.

Uri, under orders, would find the person that was to be jailed. He would detain him in a cell and provide new identification papers for him. The man's new identity would be given to Gerog, who would then provide the necessary travel visa to leave Russia.

As the trust between Uri and Gerog grew, Gerog confided to Uri how demoralized he had become with the Communist party. Uri had told Gerog that he too had reached the same conclusion that Gerog had. As a decent human being he could no longer send innocent people to their death.

The two of them developed the plan that helped so many to escape. That night, Gerog stopped on his way home and purchased a small bottle of vodka. His wife, Katrina, was shocked to see Gerog open the bottle and pour a small amount into a glass. He raised the glass and said, "I salute you, Uri Sakov, the brave hero son of Russia. May God watch over you as you enter the gates of heaven". Saying that, he downed the vodka.

As his wife watched the tears run down his face, her heart gladdened. She had not heard Gerog say the word God in over twenty years. Secretly she had never given up her faith. Maybe he still believed in God too.

Gerog walked to the sink and poured the rest of the vodka down the drain. He would never again touch another drop of alcohol.

In the spring of 1946 Gerog began preparing his last travel visas'. Gerog explained to the girls in the office that they were all going on a fact-finding mission to America. This put new life into their work. The visas would also include his wife, Katrina. Both of the secretaries had lost everyone in their families during the war. Needless to say they were excited about the prospect of going on a trip. The girls had become a big part of Katrina's and Gerog's lives. Gerog had not told them that they would not be coming back to Russia.

Travel in Russia was very difficult. So many rail lines and stations had been destroyed. Even though getting the rail lines repaired was a high-priority item progress was slow. But the Russian government put a lot of slave labor; many of them captured German prisoners, to the task of rebuilding the railroads. They died by the hundreds.

The long and arduous boat trip took almost three weeks. It was exhausting for them. But the thought of reaching America helped them endure the hardships that they encountered. Gerog decided to not let Yakov know that they were coming. He wanted to surprise Yakov and Nadya. Yakov called Rabbi Horowitz with the news and told him to meet them at the clinic. The Rabbi was delirious with joy. He yelled the news to his wife as he ran out the door. He arrived at the office just as Yakov and his family got there. The kissing and hugging and crying started all over again.

Nadya had also called Victoria Lattori. She arrived in her limousine within minutes. A City police car, with its siren screeching, had led the way. Once she was inside she became as delirious as the rest of them. When she had calmed down Victoria was on the phone making arrangements for a wonderful meal at their Sunday dinner restaurant. They all partied long into the night. To the happy foursome it all seemed like they were in a dream and at any moment they would awake and it would all be gone. But as each day melted into the next they began to feel the euphoria that only comes from being totally free.

Nadya and Yakov's delirium lasted for days. It was as if a great gift had been handed to them, and they didn't quite know what to do with it. There was so much to do to physically make mamma and poppa a part of their everyday lives. For the time being they would stay at the clinic with Yakov and Nadya. Finding a place for the two of them would come later. From the beginning of Gerog's arrival it was easy to see that he would have no trouble assimilating into this new culture. He had a thousand new questions every day. Each day he would go for a long walk. The sights, the sounds, the smells, the people—he had to experience it all as quickly as possible.

Mama Yakov, on the other hand, had approached the change quietly and cautiously. It was over a week before she even stepped out of the clinic for a breath of fresh air. She began waiting at the corner for her grandson Sergi to return from school. Sergi was now ten and the turmoil of how to deal with grand parents was a little daunting. But loving grandmothers have a way of breaking down barriers.

Sergi had become Mama's personal translator and language teacher. Nadya and Yakov had taught their son Sergi to speak Russian. Together he and momma would travel the city on foot, by bus, and the subway. He would often laugh when his grandma became excited over a new discovery. She would burst out into a long Russian tirade, laugh loudly, and hug her grandson so hard he would have to break away from her to catch his breath. She could never have imagined how magical these moments of pure joy could be while living under the absolute despair of communism. The new found breath of freedom had restored her life.

CHAPTER 20

WOMAN OF THE YEAR

Of all the events in Yakov and Nadya's lives the selection of Mary Dawson as New York City's woman of the year was one of their proudest moments. Victoria Lattori would run and hug Mary every time she came within ten feet of her. Ever since Mary had come to work for Victoria garbage had become Mary's life. The two of them made a great team in the garbage business. Don Salvatore Mancini, the mob boss of all New York City, knew a good thing when he saw it. All the under bosses thought Don Salvatore had lost his mind. He pretty much let the two women run things as they saw fit. If Mary and Victoria came up with a new idea to increase profits by cutting costs or improve efficiency they would prepare the new proposal down to the smallest detail. They would meet with the Don, hand him a copy of the proposal, and they would explain it to him. He would suggest changes, they would shake hands, and the deal was done.

One of Mary's proposals, which led to the woman of the year award, was to stop the loading of garbage on to barges, taking them out to sea, and dumping the refuse into the ocean. It was a costly way to get rid of garbage. And Mary, who had made several trips on the barges out to the dumpsite, quickly realized that it wasn't doing the ocean any good either. The water was about 250 feet deep. A lot of the garbage would float and drift miles from the dumping area. Dead marine life floated on the surface, and the stench could be smelled for miles.

Mary and Victoria proposed the idea of purchasing several land sites north of the city. These areas were already accessible by roads and consisted of land that had deep ravines. The land was pretty much useless for development of any kind. Owners of these parcels jumped at the chance to make some money. Trucking the garbage to these sites would save the Don thousands of dollars a day. A small part of the huge savingws would be used to offset the increased maintenance on the trucks. Bulldozers would be needed to compact the garbage at the bottom of the ravines.

The most unique part of the proposal was two-fold. Part one dealt with the lost revenue for the barge company. A subsidiary company of the garbage company would be set up and run by the barge owners. They would be responsible for the maintenance and replacement of all the trucks and the hiring and firing of personnel. The part that the Don liked the most was the huge tax write-off that came from leasing the trucks back from his own subsidiary. This set up increased profits for the Don enormously.

Part two of the proposal involved a deal with the City fathers. New contracts would be negotiated that included a reduction in garbage collection fees. The savings to the City amounted to $400,000 a year. There was also a secret fund set up by Victoria and Don Salvatore that was used to bribe certain city officials. The Don called it grease. The payments insured that the wheels of city government ran smoothly. Garbage had become one of the most lucrative enterprises in the Don Salvatore mob family.

On the night of the award ceremony, many people from the press corps were in attendance. Constance Higgins, a reporter from the New York Times, and her photographer, were there for the award. At the end of the ceremony Mary had to face a press conference. Connie noticed that Mary was wearing a gold pin. It was the pin that Yakov and Nadya gave to all the women after they successfully completed the rehab program. It was a simple pin that consisted of three letters joined together. YYI. It stood for the Yakov Yakov Institute. Mary wore the pin everyday to remind her how far she had come. It represented the two people that had saved her life. She shared her love and gratitude with them every day.

Connie stared at the pin and wondered what it meant.

"Miss Dawson, what does the pin on your blouse represent," asked Connie?

Connie seemed to sense that there was something significant about the pin. She had seen her wearing it in other photos of Mary just after the award was announced.

In her excitement Mary responded, "It stands for The Yakov Yakov Institute. It's one of the schools that I attended."

All of the other reporters were asking questions related to Mary's award. But not Connie. Mary's answer aroused in Connie a curiosity that wouldn't go away.

The next day, back at the paper, she began to research for this Yakov Yakov Institute. There was nothing in the paper's extensive archives. But the phone book listed a Yakov Chiropractic Clinic. That afternoon she took a cab to the clinic.

She entered the office. "Hello, may I help you," asked Sasha Carpov, the receptionist.

"Is Mary Dawson here," asked Connie?

"Not at the present time. She's probably working," responded Sasha.

"Do you know her," asked Connie?

"Yes I do. She is a dear friend of mine", said Sasha.

Connie continued her line of questioning. "Does she come here often?".

Sasha had no idea that she was being interrogated by a barracuda.

"Yes she does," said Sasha.

Just then Mary walked into the Office. Connie jumped to her feet, extended her hand and said," Hello Miss Dawson. I'm Connie Higgins, a reporter from the New York Times. We met at the award ceremony."

Mary shook her hand. In an astonished voice she said," How can I help you?"

Connie set the hook and was ready to reel her in. "I want to do a follow up story about the institute that you attended. I see your wearing your graduation pin."

"Yes, Mary said, I always wear it."

"Where exactly is this institute located," asked Connie?

Mary was floundering. "It's a small private school upstate near Syracuse," she responded. "I'm sorry Miss Higgins but I'm late for work. Please excuse me." Mary left the office totally confused about this reporter.

Connie thanked the receptionist for her help and left. Back at her office she wondered why Mary had told her the institute was in Syracuse. She found no such school in the Syracuse phone book. But she did find Dawson listed fifteen times. She began dialing asking the same question each time. "Hello. I'm Connie Higgins a reporter for the New York Times. May I speak to Mary Dawson?"

On the seventh call she got the response she had been looking for.

"No, I'm sorry Mary is not here. Can I give her a message for you? She calls me once a week from New York," said Mrs. Dawson.

"No, said Connie, but thank you. I was wondering if you know anything about the school that Mary graduated from, The Yakov Yakov Institute."

THE BREATH OF FREEDOM

In all her innocence Mary's mother replied," It's not a school. It's the clinic that saved her life. Doctor Yakov gave my Mary back to me."

"I'm doing a story about the clinic for my paper. Can you tell me where I can find this Doctor Yakov," asked Connie?

"Why yes I can. His office is at the Yakov Chiropractic Clinic," she replied.

"Thank you Mrs. Dawson. You have been a big help. I'll let you know when the story comes out", said Connie and she hung up the phone.

Mrs. Dawson immediately called Mary to tell her about the interview. She could not understand why the news made Mary so upset.

The next day Connie was determined to get to the truth. She arrived at the clinic dressed in a white doctor's coat. On her coat her name tag said she was Angela Harris from the New York City Department of Health. She carried a clipboard that added to her disguise. Most people, when they see a person carrying a clipboard, become curious. They wonder what in the world is she writing down. Connie waited outside for Sasha to leave her desk. It was her lunch hour and Sasha often ate at the diner around the corner from the clinic. She quickly entered the office and opened the door to the examination rooms' hallway. As she walked about, she would peer at something and make a check mark on the paper in the clipboard. She really looked official. No one stopped her.

She couldn't find anything unusual going on in the exam rooms in the office section of the factory. As she neared the end of the corridor she noticed a nurse standing in front of the elevator door waiting for it to open. The elevator had recently been installed. It was a big expenditure, but it made access to the second floor so much easier. The freight elevator inside the factory was not suitable for carrying people. What caught

121

Connie's eye was the pin that the nurse had on her uniform. It was the same YYI pin that she had seen Mary wearing.

"Nurse, are you a graduate of the Yakov Yakov Institute," asked Connie?

"Who are you," asked the nurse in return?

"I'm from the City Board of Health. My name is Angela Harris," replied Connie.

Just then the elevator door opened. The nurse stepped into the elevator. Just as Connie was about to step in with her, the nurse stopped her.

"I'm sorry but no one is allowed on the second floor without Doctor Yakov's permission," said the nurse. Connie didn't want to press the issue. She stepped out of the way, and the door closed. The elevator left the main floor.

Connie began looking for another way to get to the upper floor. The wall that once held the heavy cumbersome sliding door into the factory had long ago been replaced by Leonard. He had inserted a framed heavy steel door into the opening and filled in the spaces on either side of the door. Leonard had established his workshop on the factory side of the wall. He also had plenty of storage space for materials and tools. Several new exam rooms were completed but were not in use yet.

Normally the door to this section of the factory was always kept locked. But on this day Leonard was working on repairing the steps at the far end of factory that led to the second floor of the factory. He had unlocked the steel door, closed it behind him, but didn't lock it. Connie tried the doorknob, and to her surprise the door opened. She walked into the factory and closed the door. Except for the new door and three finished exam rooms not much had been done in the factory. It was dusty and dirty, but the factory windows provided plenty of light to see by. She could hear Leonard working at the far end of the building. He was unaware that she was there.

THE BREATH OF FREEDOM

As Connie walked down the middle aisle to the far end of old factory she spotted the stairs leading up to the second floor of the factory. From where he was working Leonard's view of the steps was obscured by a pile of boxes and building materials. He was totally engrossed in his work.

As she stood at the bottom of the steps she wondered if they were sturdy enough to support her. She stood on the first stair tread and tested its strength by quietly moving her weight up and down. It was very solid. Slowly she climbed the steps to the top. It brought her through the opening that was cut into the second story floor. The pungent odor of tobacco was still very strong. The dust swirled around her shoes, as she made her way toward a door in a partition that stretched across the factory. If her calculation was correct this door would lead her into the area where the new elevator opened on the second story of the factory.

As she stood at the door she noticed a stream of light coming from under door. She turned the doorknob. This door was also unlocked. She opened the door slightly and looked inside. She saw a lighted corridor. There were closed doors on both sides of the hallway. She removed her dust-covered white coat and left it behind. Connie opened the door and entered the hall. The first door on the right was the closest to her. She could hear muffled moaning on the other side of the door. Slowly she turned the door handle and opened the door a couple of inches. Nothing could have prepared her for what she was witnessing.

Doctor Nadya was standing in front of the stim machine adjusting the settings of voltage and intervals. Connie stared in disbelief as she watched the woman on the bed moving her body up and down as if she was having intercourse, convulsing and relaxing to the settings on the machine.

She had no idea what was going on. Connie burst into the room.

123

She yelled, "Stop it! You're hurting her. What are you doing to her?"

Yakov, who was in the completed room next door, heard Nadya's loud voice screaming, demanding to know who this strange woman was. Yakov turned off the machine, grabbed Connie and pulled her out into the hallway. Who are you and how did you get in here," asked Yakov?

"What are you doing to that woman," demanded Connie?

"Please calm down. I assure you Melissa is not being hurt in any way. She was experiencing very intense orgasms induce by an electronic stimulator," explained Yakov.

"Who are you and how did you get in here," Yakov asked again.

"My name is Connie Higgins. I am a reporter for The New York Times. I was at Mary Dawson's Woman of the Year party. I am writing a story about the Yakov Yakov Institute," said Connie.

"Mary was our first graduate. She was near death when we found her. She was lying on the ground outside my chiropractic office. She had been badly beaten and had lost a lot of blood," explained Yakov.

Nadya came out of the room and said to Yakov, "Melissa is stable. There was no damage done. She's fine."

"I was explaining to Connie what we do here at the institute. She's a reporter for the Times newspaper," said Yakov.

"Yes, I know who she is. How did she get in? Yakov, she will ruin everything if she is allowed to do this story. She can destroy us. We'll lose the dream that freedom has given us," said Nadya.

Yakov grabbed Nadya's arm and moved her a few feet away from the others. By this time Leonard and the nurse aiding Nadya had arrived.

THE BREATH OF FREEDOM

"I think I know a way to persuade her not to do the story," whispered Yakov.

"But how . . . ."

"Sh sh sh, trust me," he replied.

He turned to Connie and said," would you like to see how my wife's discovery works?"

Connie was stunned. This could become her greatest story. This flashed through her mind as she replied," I would love to learn all there is to know."

Yakov took her arm and escorted her to the far end of the hall, opened the first door and walked her over to the bed. The nurse Connie had met at the elevator was changing the urine stained sheets that the restrained woman in the bed was laying on. She was nude and barely conscious.

"We found this woman lying in the street in front of our office. Several of the women we have saved have come to us that way. There was an empty purse on the ground near her, and she was in a serious state of drug-withdrawal. There was an old driver's license in he purse with the name Melissa Ethridge on it. We assumed it was hers," explained Yakov.

"How long have you been doing this treatment," asked Connie?

"Since I started experimenting and developing the procedure on myself, it has been three years. Because of a medical condition that developed when our son was born I became dependent on pain narcotics. Out of desperation to save my marriage, myself, and for the sake of our son, I tried electrical stimulation of the clitoris. The treatments gradually eliminated my craving for drugs," explained Nadya.

"We don't know how it affects the brain. We only know that it works and the results are permanent with no apparent side effects," added Yakov.

125

"Are you telling me that Mary Dawson was once like this woman?" Asked Connie. "Oh no. She was much worse. Mary had been so badly beaten that she suffered from amnesia for several weeks. As she went through the treatments the swelling in her brain gradually reduced. You can't imagine the joy we shared on the day she remembered her name," explained Nadya

"Donna, will you prepare the patient for her first treatment," asked Yakov?

Everyone in the room looked at each other wondering if Yakov had gone mad or something. "Donna has been with us for two years. She decided to become a nurse after she had completed her treatments. Out of gratitude she has stayed on with us. Doctor Yakov has trained her in administering the procedure. We love her, and the way the other women relate to her is amazing," said Yakov.

Donna hooked up the electrodes. She carefully placed the first electrode into the vagina next to the clitoris. The second one Donna taped to an area that had been shaved at the base of the skull.

She looked at Nadya and said," I'm ready doctor."

"Turn it on," replied Nadya.

As the light voltage passed into her body Connie saw a slight upward thrust of the patient's pelvic area. The short interval passed and her body relaxed. After ten applications of the voltage the machine was turned off, and she was allowed to rest.

"This is how we begin the treatments. Very gradually over the course of six to eight weeks the voltage is increased and the interval time is shortened. Once the patient is able to fully understand what is being done to her and for her, Donna carefully explains what is happening. At this point the patient is given the choice of stopping the treatment or going the full course. No one has ever said stop," explained Nadya.

THE BREATH OF FREEDOM

"They are never in any pain, added Donna. I can't begin to describe the intense euphoric sensation that the orgasms produce. Your mind becomes clearer and sharper than it has ever been as the craving for drugs disappears. It's like reentering the world as a whole human being. The Yakovs saved my life."

Connie could not believe what she had just witnessed. She held her head in her hands and sobbed uncontrollably. Nadya wrapped her arms around her and waited for her to stop crying. She could not understand this response to what she had just witnessed.

As she gained control again she turned and looked deeply into Nadya's eyes and said," I want to be whole again. I have become a drug addict. Heroin is destroying me. I thought it would help me to deal with the huge pressures of being a top reporter. Instead my using has ruined everything. Will you help me? I beg you. Save me from my own destruction."

Yakov wrapped his arms around the two women and said," I saw the signs that alerted me to your addiction. Of course we will help you. I just want you to know you will be the first patient that starts the program in a fully conscious condition," he said. Everyone in the room laughed.

"We only ask that you never reveal to anyone what you will experience. Wear your YYI pin proudly. Let it remind you everyday what a great thing that you have accomplished. You will share a special bond with all of our girls and us that you chose life over a living death. Just as Nadya and I chose the breath of freedom over the fear of death and despair, you too have made the same choice.

The End

Salvatore Paolucci
709 Eastlake Drive
Edwardsville, Illinois 62025
salpao@sbcglobal.net
618-656-8076

CPSIA information can be obtained at www.ICGtesting.com
Printed in the USA
LVOW072355301111

257234LV00001B/2/P